THE FIVE ANCESTORS
OUT OF THE ASHES
Book 1

PHOENIX

The Five Ancestors

The Five Ancestors
OUT OF THE ASHES

THE FIVE ANCESTORS
OUT OF THE ASHES
Book 1

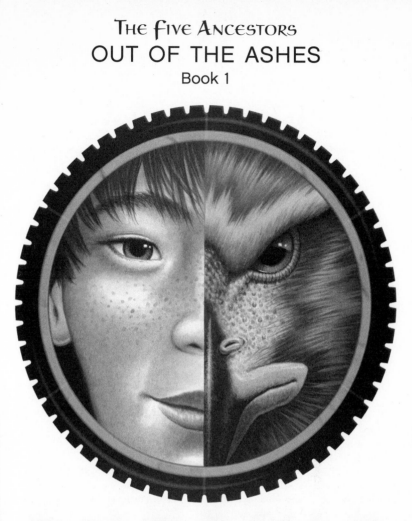

PHOENIX

JEFF STONE

Random House New York

Text copyright © 2012 by Jeffrey S. Stone
Jacket art copyright © 2012 by Richard Cowdrey

Visit us on the Web! randomhouse.com/kids

Educators and librarians, for a variety of teaching tools, visit us at
RHTeachersLibrarians.com

Library of Congress Cataloging-in-Publication Data
Stone, Jeff.
Phoenix / Jeff Stone. — 1st ed.
  p. cm. — (Five ancestors: out of the ashes ; bk. 1)
Summary: "When their home is robbed, thirteen-year-old Phoenix Collins, an up-and-coming amateur mountain-bike racer, discovers a shocking mystery about his grandfather, and Phoenix must travel to China and then to Texas to find some answers." — Provided by publisher.
ISBN 978-0-375-87018-7 (trade) — ISBN 978-0-375-97018-4 (lib. bdg.) —
ISBN 978-0-375-98759-5 (ebook)
[1. Bicycle motocross—Fiction. 2. Adventure and adventurers—Fiction.
3. Supernatural—Fiction. 4. Grandfathers—Fiction. 5. Orphans—Fiction.
6. China—Fiction. 7. Texas—Fiction.] I. Title.
PZ7.S87783Pho 2012 [Fic]—dc23 2012006607

Printed in the United States of America
10 9 8 7 6 5 4 3 2 1
First Edition

Random House Children's Books supports the First Amendment
and celebrates the right to read.

For Coach Bob Brooks.
Tag.
You're it.

THE FIVE ANCESTORS
OUT OF THE ASHES
Book 1

PHOENIX

STAGE ONE

FIRST RULE OF CYCLING
Never Blame the Bike

The pistol fired, and I hammered my feet down. My mountain bike shot forward like a bullet.

Elbows and knees flew in every direction as we raced, the other riders and I jockeying to be first onto the narrow dirt single-track. This was Town Run Trail Park, after all, not some perfectly groomed thirty-foot-wide BMX track. The route was a single lane over eight twisting miles of Indiana hardwoods and dried creek beds. It was nearly impossible to pass anyone in the tangle of low branches and exposed tree roots coming up, so commanding the lead at the beginning was crucial.

It took me less than fifteen seconds to shake the pack and hit the trailhead first. Disappearing into the trees, I leaned into the initial turn, feeling the wind through the vents in my battered helmet. Tree limbs bounced off my cracked goggles and duct-taped face mask, and thorny vines tore at my shin guards. My gloved knuckles smacked against massive tree trunks as my bike rocked from side to side on my push to increase my lead.

I attacked the single-track like an animal.

Like a wolf.

Like a cheetah.

Predator, not prey.

Back in the pack, you must outrun whatever is closest at your heels. Out front, it's you against the trail. You have to attack it, or it will attack you.

Thirty seconds into the race, I was so far ahead that the others couldn't even see my shadow. I whipped around a bend and saw the trail's first climb. I shifted to the smallest sprocket on my rear wheel cassette and hit the dirt slope like a salmon swimming upstream.

My back tire began to fishtail violently, and I leaned out over the handlebars to get better balance and more traction. It was hard work. Most guys gave up at this point and simply jumped off their bike. They unclipped their feet from their quick-release pedals, shouldered their ride, and ran like a mountain goat. The trouble was, clipping back in at the top of the hill took time.

I didn't have any time to lose, so I kept cranking. This was a race, after all. It didn't matter that it was only a small-time event. Losing wasn't an option.

I *hate* to lose.

I continued up the hill until I crested the rise; then I picked the cleanest line down the back side and hurled onward. As gravity sucked me down the rear slope, I stopped pedaling to conserve energy. I was going to need it. Ahead was the trail's most dangerous section.

When I reached the end of the downhill run, I gently squeezed my index fingers over my brake levers, slowing. The trail had been dry so far, but the low ground looming before me harbored water overflowing from the White River mere yards away. Half an inch of turbid liquid floated atop several inches of muck. I flicked my right thumb, changing to an easier gear, and continued forward.

I motored into the rank sludge and immediately felt my hip flexor muscles begin to burn from the effort. The muck threatened to suck my tires right off the rims. Crud flew up in every direction as my rear wheel splattered a black line straight up my back, my front wheel slinging gelatinous clumps of earth up under my face mask and across the front of my goggles.

When I was halfway across the muck meadow, I heard a splash. I glanced over my shoulder, expecting to see a deer or maybe a raccoon.

It was neither. It was another rider.

I knew most of the dozen other racers, but I didn't recognize this kid. He was a beast. His forearms were as thick as baseball bats, and the thighs bulging beneath his three-hundred-dollar skin suit looked as if they had been transplanted from an Olympic speed skater. I remembered seeing him at the starting line but had dismissed him as another aspiring muscle head wanting to race mountain bikes as a means of improving his cardio for other sports.

He was probably fifteen years old, the maximum age for this race bracket and two years older than I was. I'd assumed his expensive racing kit and full-suspension ultra-lightweight carbon bike had little to do with actual skill and more to do with rich parents.

But I was wrong. Whoever was behind that mirrored face mask could ride.

I shook my head. I'd never been very good at riding through water, and I needed to focus. I didn't want to risk taking a dip in the bacteria soup surrounding me now. I decided to keep my pace slow and steady while the other kid pushed recklessly forward, water rooster-tailing off his bike like a wake behind a speedboat.

Unfortunately, his strategy worked better than mine. By the time my tires found firm ground, he was on top of me.

Literally.

The trail was slightly wider here, but it was littered with gnarled roots rising up out of the ground. This stretch was difficult to traverse solo, and potentially deadly if one rider tried to pass another.

The kid wanted to pass.

I wasn't about to let him.

"Move it!" he snarled.

I held my ground.

He reached out and grabbed the back of my jersey, tugging violently. I had to hit my brakes to keep from getting pulled off my bike.

He let go and shot past me.

Crap. That wasn't only illegal, it was incredibly dangerous. I flicked my thumb, changed gears, and began to hammer. My main strength is sprinting, and I caught him in seconds. The trail was still root-ridden, and it rattled my bones down to the marrow, but I didn't care.

"On your left!" I shouted, knowing full well that he wouldn't heed my request to pass on that side. He cut over to his left, and I made a move to pass him on the right.

He saw me coming and cut his wheel sharply back over to the right, slamming into me. I absorbed the impact instead of resisting it, like water flowing around a rock. I didn't go down.

So the kid tried a different approach. He threw an elbow.

This blow caught me off guard. It struck me below the rib cage, nearly knocking the wind out of me. He cocked his arm for another swing, and I reacted without thinking. I stopped pedaling, twisted my left heel outward—freeing my shoe from its pedal clip—and kicked him in the thigh.

Hard.

He went down like a house imploding. He turtled into a ball and bounced over the rough ground, shouting a string of obscenities. Fortunately, there were no trees near enough for him to collide with, despite all the roots, and he and his bike eventually skidded to a halt.

Amazingly, in the blink of an eye he righted his bike and began to climb back on, still swearing. He appeared to be fine.

I put the hammer down once more. I pulled well ahead and reached the end of the roots, grateful that the nerve-numbing section was over. However, as soon as I was on smoother ground, I noticed that my bike didn't feel right. The front wheel seemed spongy.

Bike parts rattled loose over those roots all the time, but this was different. My front wheel began to wobble, and I tickled my brake levers to reduce my speed. The last thing I wanted was for the front wheel to—

Crunch!

My bike stopped, but my body kept moving forward. I instinctively twisted my heels outward, my shoes ripping free of the pedals as I sailed over the handlebars. With my arms outstretched like Superman, I face-planted into the dirt. My worn chinstrap snapped, and my masked helmet bounced down the trail.

I sat up and spat. Wiping my sweaty brow, I quickly checked myself over. My chin was a little sore, but otherwise I was fine.

I looked back at my bike and frowned. The front wheel had tacoed, the rim folded almost completely in half. It took a special kind of problem for that to occur. I crawled over to my bike and checked the front spokes. Several were loose. I wiped a section of the rim clean and saw that a few of the spokes had come loose from the wheel when it folded in half, but others had fresh tool marks on the spoke nuts.

Someone had loosened them.

I heard the familiar hum of bike tires on dirt, and I glanced back up the trail to see the huge kid coming on like a locomotive. He shouted, "Get that rusted piece of junk off the trail!"

I hurried to my feet. Leaving a broken bike on the

trail was dangerous for everyone, including me. That mountain of flesh might hit it and crash into me. I bent over, grabbing my bike with both hands, when the maniac roared like a lion, unclipped his foot, and unleashed a powerful kick at my face.

The reinforced toe of his mountain biking shoe caught me square on the jaw, and I blacked out.

I woke to a thick haze obscuring my vision. I was groggy, and everything I saw and heard came distorted and slow, as if my brain were floating in molasses. I felt fingers dance over my skull and across the back of my neck, and I realized I was lying flat on my back, my head cradled in my grandfather's bony hands.

"Do not move," Grandfather said. "Do not speak. Blink your eyes if you can understand me."

I blinked.

"Very good, Phoenix," Grandfather said. "Lie still while I examine you."

I did as I was told. Grandfather wasn't a doctor, but he knew more about healing than anyone I'd ever met, including my uncle Tí, who really was a doctor.

I tried to look around, but the only thing I could see was the vague outline of tree limbs dangling above me over the bike trail. It was early June, the first Saturday of summer vacation, and the foliage was thick. I doubted anyone had seen the cheap shot I took, which was fine with me.

Grandfather's face came into view, and I watched him toss his long gray ponytail braid over his shoulder as he moved his black eyes to within an inch of my own. I could smell sweat on his cheeks. He must have run all the way here from the starting line. His sweat had a peculiar odor, which I attributed to the vast quantity of dried Chinese herbs he consumed. It wasn't a bad smell, just sort of old and musty.

His gaze locked on mine, and I could tell he was checking my pupils for dilation and signs of concussion. He soon nodded, seemingly satisfied, then ran a yellowed fingernail over my bruised jaw. I flinched in pain, and he shook his head. I was not looking forward to explaining what had happened.

Punches and kicks, and the skills required to heal damage from them, were a big part of Grandfather's life, which meant they were a big part of my life. He'd raised me ever since my parents died in a car wreck when I was a baby. He was some kind of kung fu master, though he wouldn't admit it. I knew very little about him, in fact. To call him secretive would be an understatement, but he was very good to me.

I heard a bike approaching but couldn't see who it was.

"Close your eyes," Grandfather said.

I did so, grateful. The last thing I wanted now was a group conversation. It would be better to wait until I was alone with Grandfather before I shared the story of the race. He was going to be upset, and I didn't want anyone else to hear the tongue-lashing I was bound to receive. They wouldn't understand. None of them practiced kung fu.

When most people thought of kung fu, they envisioned bald Chinese guys in orange robes fighting with one another. While this is one element, there is so much more.

Kung fu actually means "accomplishment through effort," and a person can apply its philosophies to anything, not just martial arts. They don't even have to be Chinese to do it. I'm a good example. I'm only half-Chinese, but I try to live and breathe kung fu like the most hard-core monks living atop China's tallest mountains do. I try to put one hundred percent of my effort into everything every day, whether it is martial arts, mountain biking, or homework. That's what it means to be a kung fu practitioner.

I've been practicing kung fu ever since I could walk. Thanks to all that hard work, nobody could touch me on a mountain bike. Core strength exercises are the foundation of many martial arts, and they also happen to be the foundation for elite professional cyclists. Riding a bicycle involves far more than just your legs. If your torso and hips are powerful, it makes your legs exponentially stronger. Kung fu made me unstoppable on a bike.

Until now, that is.

Today I'd been beaten. It didn't matter that I'd gotten kicked in the face or that someone had tampered with my bike. Cheaters were everywhere. As a student of kung fu, I needed to overcome any obstacle, *especially* if cheating was involved.

Grandfather exuded strength, which is why I felt like such a weakling for lying here now. As he rested my head on the ground and continued the injury probe, I couldn't help but think about our similarities and differences. He was tall and thin, and he always stood ramrod straight. His hair was long, gray, and very thick, and he usually wore it pulled back in a heavy braid. He stood out in a crowd.

I stood out, too, but for different reasons. My mother had been from China, like Grandfather, while my straight-out-of-the-cornfields-of-Indiana father had been a redhead. The end result was that I have Asian facial features topped off with ratty brown hair that has a distinctly reddish tinge. I also have freckles and bright green eyes. I am of average height, and to see me walking down the street, you probably wouldn't guess that I'm an athlete, unlike the heavily muscled kid who kicked me. While muscular people can dominate in certain sports, that physique generally doesn't translate into a podium finish in cycling, because riding a bike most often comes down to power-to-weight ratio. When people think of cyclists, they don't think Arnold Schwarzenegger. They think Lance Armstrong.

I'm built like a bird, strong and light as a feather. It is Chinese tradition that a woman's father names her son, and Grandfather couldn't have picked a better name for me—Phoenix. Grandfather was amazing in so many ways. He'd given up his life in China to move to Indiana and take care of me. I couldn't even take care of my bike.

What had gone wrong?

I went through a mental checklist. I'd given my bike a complete physical two nights ago and hadn't ridden it since. I hadn't left my bike unattended here at the trail park. No one else besides Grandfather had even touched my bike in the last forty-eight hours.

Unless . . .

It was a stretch, but there had been two guys in our backyard when I'd come home from school yesterday. Two men in white disposable jumpsuits were taking soil samples from the septic field in our yard, the area where the wastewater tank for our house was buried. A van in the driveway had EPA—ENVIRONMENTAL PROTEC-TION AGENCY stenciled on the sides.

The men were such an odd pair that I watched them as they packed up and hurried off. One guy seemed average in every way except for the way he moved. He had the precise movements of a martial artist. Grandfather moved like that.

As for the other guy, he would have put the kid who kicked me to shame in the muscle department. He was a freak. I remembered thinking that he should have been inspected *by* the EPA, not working for them. It looked as if he'd been pumped with so many chemicals, he probably glowed in the dark. I even made up nicknames for these guys: Slim and Meathead.

There was something else, too. Slim was Chinese. He looked Asian, and I overheard him as he talked on a cell phone. My Chinese is rudimentary at best, and I only caught a few words, but it was definitely Mandarin Chinese.

I'd planned to ask Grandfather about these guys, but he had been napping when I'd gone into the house. He probably didn't even know they were there. When Grandfather was awake, his senses were keener than those of anyone I've ever met. When he was sleeping, however, he was dead to the world.

I'd meant to mention the guys to Grandfather after he woke up, but I forgot. It had been the last day of school, and there were more important things on my mind—like today's race.

"Open your eyes," Grandfather said, bringing me back to the present.

I opened my eyes and found the molasses around my brain beginning to thin. I saw that Grandfather was now standing, and beside him was my best friend, Jake.

Jake was the same age as I was, and we went to the same school. He had shaggy blond hair and a pug nose, and he was a great rider. He was the one who had gotten me interested in racing bikes. If it weren't for me, he'd have a roomful of first-place trophies instead of second-place ones, but he didn't seem to mind. He was cool like that.

Jake was straddling his bike, his usual baggy riding clothes flopping in the warm breeze. I was glad he was here. Grandfather might hold back on some of the verbal abuse I was bound to receive.

Grandfather leaned over and stretched a hand out

toward me. I took it, and he jerked me to my feet. I must have received a clean bill of health. Otherwise, he would have been more gentle.

Grandfather let go of my hand and walked over to my broken bicycle. He hoisted the twenty-eight-pound machine onto his shoulder as though it weighed no more than a woman's purse, and nodded at the tacoed wheel. "Is this the result of mechanical failure?"

I nodded. "You could say that."

"You should be more careful. Take care of your bicycle, and it will take care of you."

"Yes, Grandfather."

He pointed to my aching jaw. "Would you like to tell me about that?"

"Not really. I let my guard down. I've suffered the consequences. I've learned a valuable lesson."

"I hope so," Grandfather snapped. "Meet me in the parking lot." He turned and began to walk back up the trail, carrying the bike.

When Grandfather was out of earshot, Jake whistled softly. "Whoa, your grandfather sure is harsh, bro."

I shrugged.

Jake glanced down at his handlebars, and I noticed a battered helmet hanging there—my helmet. He tossed it to me.

"I showed your skid lid to your grandfather while you were unconscious," Jake said. "I told him it was trashed and that you probably cracked your skull after it flew off. I wondered if he should keep his hands off your melon in case you had, like, brain damage or something, but he must have guessed my thoughts because he pointed to your chin. What's up with that?"

I saw the concern on Jake's face and decided to tell him what had happened.

"My grandfather was right," I said. "My head is fine. I fell off my bike and another rider kicked me in the jaw. I went out like a light."

"No way! You mean that huge kid who was decked out in like ten grand worth of gear?"

"That's the one."

"He passed me early," Jake said, "elbowed me on a turn and put me in third place behind the two of you."

"He elbowed me, too. I was beating him, though, until my front wheel tacoed and I endoed over the bars. He rode up behind me, and as I bent down to move my bike, he blasted me with the kick."

"Ouch." Jake shook his head. "What are you going to do about it?"

"Nothing. It's my own fault. Even my grandfather agrees. That's why he's being so cold."

"You must have knocked a few screws loose, bro. You're not to blame."

"You don't get it," I said. "The bike broke because of a mechanical failure. My spokes were loose. It was my fault for not checking them before the race. That was my first mistake. After that kid elbowed me, I kicked him clean off his bike. I should've been ready for repercussions. My bad."

"Ahhhh, soooo," Jake joked in a cheesy Chinese accent, "kung fu master must never let guard down. Right, Grasshopper?"

I rolled my eyes. "Something like that."

"If you're all right, we'd better get going. Everyone is worried about you. Your grandfather asked all the parents to stay back at the starting line until he had a chance to look you over, but I have a feeling some of them are coming down here, anyway. A few of the moms were pretty freaked out when I rode up there to get him."

"You went to get help?"

Jake nodded. "I was ahead of the pack and found you here, out cold. I turned around and stopped the other riders, then rode back to the starting line. I found your grandfather and he ran down here almost as fast as I could ride. He may look older than dirt, but he runs like a gazelle. No offense."

"None taken," I said. "Have you seen the kid who knocked me out? Did he finish the race?"

"He probably will soon. It looks like the jerk kept riding. There are fresh tracks continuing up the trail. I assumed he was ahead of you when you wrecked, and that he didn't know you'd gone down. He's too far away to call back now. I hope they don't count the results of this race in our season total."

"They won't. He'll be the only finisher. It will give him bragging rights, though."

Up the trail, Grandfather called out, "Are you coming or not, Grasshopper?"

I felt myself begin to blush, and Jake whistled softly

again. "Harsh, bro," he said in a low voice. "Totally harsh. He's got some good ears, though."

"He's not so bad." Then I yelled, "Be right there!"

As I turned and headed for Grandfather, Jake whispered, "I'm *so* glad my parents don't have ears like that. I would never be able to get away with anything."

I hurried back up the trail on foot while Jake rode at my side. It didn't take us long to catch Grandfather. Jake waved goodbye and cruised up the single-track as I held out my broken helmet to Grandfather, intending to swap it for my broken bike.

"I will continue to carry the bicycle," Grandfather said. "It has given you enough trouble for one day."

"What happened is not the bike's fault," I said, feeling like a white belt who has failed to pass his rank promotion test. "I'm to blame. I should carry it."

"I am glad you realize who is responsible," Grandfather said. "Even so, I will carry it. You were unconscious. You may become dizzy again."

"Thank you, Grandfather."

He nodded.

We rounded a bend, and I saw a group of adults that included Jake's dad hanging out on the trail. Jake was with them. Jake's dad called out, "Phoenix! Are you okay? We came down to see if we could help, but you seemed to already be in good hands. Who knew your grandfather could move so fast?"

"I'm fine," I called back. "Just a bit of a headache. Jake was a big help. I appreciate you all coming down here, but we're heading back now."

"All right," Jake's dad replied, "glad to hear you're okay. We'll see you in the parking lot."

Jake's dad retreated with the group in tow. I stopped and waited. Grandfather stopped, too, no doubt sensing that I wanted to talk about something. I wanted to tell him about Slim and Meathead.

"Grandfather," I said when the others were out of earshot, "did you happen to see a Chinese man this morning, or a big bodybuilder guy?"

"No. Should I have?"

"I don't think so."

"Then why do you ask?"

"They were out at our house yesterday while you were asleep. I forgot to tell you about it. Then today, my front wheel falls apart. I know I should have checked it this morning before the race, but it was fine on Thursday night. At some point between then and now, someone loosened my spokes. There are fresh tool marks on the spoke nuts. For some reason, I think those guys might be responsible."

"That makes no sense, Phoenix. What were they doing at our home?"

"Taking soil samples from our septic field. They looked for real. They even had an EPA van."

Grandfather raised a bushy eyebrow. "That is strange. I thought those agencies leave some type of notice that they have been on someone's property. How do you know one was Chinese?"

"I heard him speaking on a cell phone."

"What did he say?"

I looked down at my feet. "I, uh, didn't hear well enough."

Grandfather began to walk again, quickly. I looked up and followed. He was moving fast.

"I do not like the sound of this," he said. "Where was your bicycle yesterday?"

"On the back porch, where I always leave it. It was locked to the railing, but anyone with a spoke wrench could have tampered with the front wheel. It would have only taken a few minutes."

"Why do you think someone might do this?"

"I don't know. Maybe they wanted me to lose."

Grandfather rubbed his long chin with his free hand. "Or perhaps they wanted to sabotage your bicycle in order to create a distraction. They somehow knew you would be racing this morning, and that I would be with you. If you were injured, we would be at the hospital for hours."

"I don't understand," I said. "What is going on?"

"I do not know, but I can make a guess. This may not be about you at all, Phoenix. It may be about me. We have to hurry. I am afraid those men you saw may attempt to break into our home."

We reached the parking lot just after Jake's father and the other adults. We headed for our old Ford Ranger pickup, and I noticed someone leaning against the pickup's hood. It was the kid who'd kicked me in the face. He turned in my direction, and my jaw dropped. I knew him.

His name was Ryan Vanderhausen. His rich uncle blew more money on equipment and training for him than most families earned in a year. Ryan had spent the past semester with his uncle in Belgium, where cycling was more like a religion than a sport. It wasn't unheard of for riders to get a lot better, or athletes to gain a lot more muscle, by training hard, but what I saw out on the trail and standing before me now was unreal. I could hardly believe this was the same kid Jake and I had smoked time and again last year. Ryan was fourteen then, which meant he was fifteen now, but there was no way a normal kid could have grown that much in a single semester.

I looked over at Jake. His eyes were as big as mine. Jake's dad whispered something to him, and they headed to their minivan, shaking their heads. They were probably thinking the same thing I was. *What on earth happened to Ryan?*

"Ryan?" Grandfather asked.

Ryan smirked but said nothing.

From behind Grandfather's truck came a tall, thin man wearing a full road bike racing kit. The man's riding shorts and short-sleeved jersey were skintight, and his legs were shaved. His brilliant white socks glowed against his deep "roadie" tan, and he had on one of those silly little hats with the tiny brim that bike racers wore in the old days beneath their leather riding helmets. Somehow, though, he still managed to look dignified.

I knew exactly who he was—Dr. Vanderhausen, Ryan's uncle. "Dr. V," as he liked to be called, looked almost exactly like Ryan's father, which was eerie. Ryan's dad had died of cancer last November. I'd met Dr. V at the funeral. He was a chemist, and he'd gotten rich by developing a diet drug. He'd sold his company for hundreds of millions of dollars and was now enjoying an early retirement.

"Phoenix Collins!" Dr. V said with a cheerful Belgian accent. "Chinese first name, Indiana last name. I remember you. You still look as unique as ever. I bet the girls go crazy over those green eyes."

I didn't reply. For some reason, Dr. V gave me the creeps.

"I'm sorry that you didn't finish the race," Dr. V continued. "I understand you are normally the man to beat. What happened? Did you have some sort of accident?"

I felt color rising in my cheeks, and I glared at Ryan. I'd always considered him a friend until now. He was an aggressive rider, sure, but he would never have kicked or elbowed Jake or me before spending all that time with his uncle.

I looked at Dr. V. "Why don't you ask your nephew what happened?"

"Me?" Ryan asked coyly. "I have no idea what you're talking about. I blew past you after the root section, and that was the last I saw of you or anyone else. It's not my fault you can't keep up with me anymore."

I ground my teeth, and I felt Grandfather place his hand on my shoulder. "We should leave," he said.

"Just a moment, sir," Dr. V said to Grandfather. "Please excuse my rudeness. Greetings to you. I trust you recall we met at my brother's wake. Allow me to assist." He raised his arms to take my bike from Grandfather's shoulder, but I rushed forward to take it.

Dr. V stepped aside and grinned. "I would never let anyone touch my bike as a boy, either. I see that you ride a rigid aluminum frame, Phoenix. How . . . traditional. Have you ever tried full suspension?"

"You mean like Ryan's five-thousand-dollar carbon bike with more shocks than wheels?" I asked, unable to stop my sarcasm. Dr. V was really bugging me. "I don't think so."

I walked to the bike rack attached to our pickup truck's trailer hitch and began to secure my four-hundred-dollar bicycle. I could never afford a bike like Ryan's.

Dr. V stepped around the truck. "Actually, Ryan's bike frame is made of magnesium, not carbon fiber, and it cost twelve thousand dollars. It's state-of-the-art feather-weight technology. Nothing but the best for my team members. You could ride one, too, if you play your cards right."

I stopped. "Huh?"

"Have you ever heard of cyclocross?"

I tried not to roll my eyes. Of course I'd heard of cyclocross. People race road bikes outfitted with mountain bike–type knobby tires over manmade courses that contain obstacles such as wooden barriers and sand pits. Sometimes they even race in snow. It's ridiculous.

"Cyclocross is essentially steeplechase on bicycles," I said.

"That's right," Dr. V replied. "I formed a European cyclocross team last year, Team Vanderhausen. Our slogan is 'V equals Victory.' To be honest, we didn't do so well, so I've built a cutting-edge training facility here in the United States in Texas Hill Country, just outside of Austin. I'm recruiting new talent to try our luck on the American circuit. Ryan and I are flying down there tomorrow and we'll be there all summer, preparing for the autumn cyclocross season. Would you be interested in coming down to train with us for a month or two? I am curious to see if you're as good as everyone says. They say you are as fast as an adult. I will pay all of your expenses, of course."

"What?" Ryan said indignantly, pushing himself away from the truck. "You never told me this. You want me to ride with *him*? No way!"

Dr. V looked at Ryan. "Afraid of a little competition? I would have thought those vitamins you've been taking lately had grown some hair on your chest, along with all of those muscles."

Ryan looked as though he'd been slapped in the face. He stormed off. I saw a large woman climb out of an expensive sedan and begin to hurry after him. It was his mother. She caught up with Ryan and tried to put an arm around him, but he shoved her away, a look of disgust in his eyes.

Ryan was being a total jerk. His mom had always been nice to Jake and me. I'd never seen Ryan act like this before, to her or anyone else.

Dr. V looked at Grandfather and shrugged. "Irritable teens," Dr. V said. "What can you do?"

Grandfather said nothing. He removed the truck keys from the pants pocket of his sweat suit and opened the driver's-side door. I finished securing my bike to the rack and headed for the passenger side.

"Well?" Dr. V asked me. "Are you interested?"

Part of me was flattered that he'd given me an invitation, but I had no interest in riding cyclocross. It was a silly sport. Even worse, Dr. V was creepy.

"No, thanks," I said, climbing into the truck.

Dr. V reached into one of the water bottle pockets sewn into the back of his riding jersey and pulled out a business card. He handed the card to Grandfather and said, "This is a once-in-a-lifetime opportunity."

Grandfather glanced at the card, then handed it to me. I could tell that he already sensed how I felt about the offer.

"Would you like to go to Texas this summer, Phoenix?" Grandfather asked.

"Nope," I replied. "Too hot."

Grandfather started the truck and nodded to Dr. V. "Thank you for your kind offer, but I am afraid my grandson has declined. We must go now."

Dr. V opened his mouth to say something more, but Grandfather dropped the transmission into drive and spun the wheel, peeling out of the parking lot.

5

I breathed a sigh of relief as our small pickup truck raced down the road. I was glad to be away from Dr. V, and from Ryan. I still couldn't believe how much Ryan had changed on the outside, as well as the inside. While he was never a good friend, I did go over to his house a couple of times with Jake to hang out. Ryan wasn't disrespectful toward his mother then like he was today. In fact, he was so tight with his parents that I really envied him.

When Ryan's dad died, Grandfather took Jake and me to the funeral. Ryan seemed to appreciate that we were there, but we didn't know what to say to him. Ryan's dad and Dr. V had been elite cyclists when they were young, so Jake and I mostly just stood around and listened to the other cyclists who had come to pay their respects. There had been a lot of whispering about whether Ryan would keep riding without his father. Clearly, he had, and while he was in Belgium, he'd obviously taken it to a whole new level. He was different now, though, and I was certain that Dr. V was responsible.

I turned to Grandfather to talk with him about Ryan, but Grandfather was lost in his own thoughts, so I let him be. I pressed my palms against the dashboard, feeling anxious about what we might find at home. We lived only a few miles from Town Run Trail Park, and the way Grandfather was driving, we would be there in a couple of minutes.

Like Town Run Trail Park, our house was situated along the White River. The home was tiny, but the property was pretty big. It was several acres and there were tons of trees. Maple and oak covered the high ground at the front, while birch and scrub cedar grew in the swampy rear where the land dipped down to the river. It was beautiful and secluded, and from the house you couldn't see the road or any of the neighbors. It was perfect for Grandfather's secretive nature, but all those trees might be a problem now. If someone was inside our house, no one would know it.

"Maybe we should stop somewhere and call the police," I said. "Too bad we don't have a cell phone."

Grandfather shook his head. "Let us see what there is to see, first. I do not want the authorities to think that I am a paranoid old man if there is no trouble."

I wasn't sure I agreed, but I kept my mouth shut. I shifted in my seat, a million questions running through my mind. The main one was, *What could we possibly have in our house that was worth stealing?* I wanted to ask Grandfather about this and many more things, but I knew I wouldn't get any answers. I was becoming convinced he was hiding something. Deep down, I'd suspected this for a very long time. The only thing I really knew about him was his name, *Chénjí Long*, or "Silent Dragon" in Mandarin Chinese. It was a perfect name for someone as tight-lipped as he was.

We turned onto our gravel driveway, and Grandfather wove quickly past the overgrown trees lining the drive. He surprised me by stomping on the brakes a full fifty yards from the house. This was where the trees stopped and the lawn began. I didn't see any vehicles anywhere.

"Stay in the truck," Grandfather ordered.

Before I could argue, he cut the engine and slipped out the driver's-side door. He hurried across the yard, toward our house.

It took me a few seconds to figure out what he was up to. By parking here, he blocked the only exit for vehicles that might be out of view.

Grandfather reached the front door, and I watched him turn the handle without inserting a key. Unbelievably, the door opened. That door was always locked. This was serious.

Grandfather entered the house, and I couldn't take it anymore. I got out of the truck and was heading across the drive when I heard a tremendous *CRASH!*

I rushed toward the house and heard what sounded like someone chopping wood inside. The chopping stopped as I reached the open door.

I poked my head through the doorway, into the family room, but didn't see anyone. I stepped inside, and my heart sank. Our home had been ransacked. We didn't have a lot of things, but what we did own looked as though a tornado had ravaged it. Our furniture had been slit open. Pillows had been slashed, and feathers drifted through the room like dandelion fluff. In the kitchen, our table and chairs were upended. The contents of every cupboard and drawer seemed to be on the floor, the drawers themselves among the mess.

Grandfather gave a muffled cry, and my heart nearly stopped. The sound came from his bedroom.

I knew that if I was going to help him, I needed a weapon. I considered going into the garage to grab something from our practice weapons rack, but it would take too long.

I was still wearing my mountain biking cleats, which were similar to the cleats worn by soccer players. They also had a large metal bracket mounted on the bottom at the ball of the foot for clipping into pedals. Those brackets were serious chunks of metal. I took off my shoes, letting them dangle loosely in my grip, and slunk down the hallway toward Grandfather's bedroom.

His door was open. Just inside the doorway was the hulking back of a man who was holding Grandfather in a tight bear hug. All I could see of Grandfather was his legs. His feet were off the ground and he was writhing like a snake, but he couldn't seem to break free.

Beyond Grandfather, I caught a glimpse of an ax head swinging through the air. There was a loud *CHOP*, and the back of Grandfather's overturned armoire splintered. The man holding the ax was Slim. The other man had to be Meathead.

I lunged at Meathead from his blind side, swinging a shoe with all my might. The metal bracket struck him behind the ear, and the huge man dropped to his knees.

The shoe fell from my hand as Grandfather slipped free.

I stepped around Meathead and shouted, "Look out, Grandfather!"

Slim had raised the ax and was coming at us. I hurled my other shoe at Slim's face just as Grandfather dove at Slim's raised arms.

Grandfather managed to knock the ax free of Slim's hands, but my flying shoe struck Grandfather in the side of the head, and he went down.

"No!" I shouted.

I took a step toward Slim and felt an arm wrap around my neck from behind like a boa constrictor. It was Meathead. He was still conscious. The giant began to squeeze. I felt pressure build in my head as Meathead's forearm pressed against the side of my neck, compressing my carotid artery and cutting off the flow of blood to my brain. A flash of bright white light exploded behind my eyes, and for the second time in less than an hour, I blacked out.

When I came to, I found myself atop what remained of my bed. Like the furniture in our family room, my mattress had been sliced to ribbons. Grandfather was sitting in a dining chair beside me.

"Phoenix," he said. "How do you feel?"

"Like someone tried to hang me with a noose," I groaned, rubbing my neck. I tried to sit up, but felt dizzy and lay back down. "Ugh. How are you?"

Grandfather pointed to a large lump beneath his long gray hair. "Perhaps you should consider giving baseball a try. You have a strong throw."

"I'm so sorry, Grandfather."

"No need to apologize. You had the right idea, only I got in the way."

"I still feel bad that I hit you. Did I knock you out?"

"You did. It seems they incapacitated you, too. The

bruising on your neck leads me to believe it was a choke hold."

"Yeah, the big guy was still conscious. He latched on to me after you went down. Are my bruises bad?"

"The bruising is fine. You can rub it out later with some *dit da jow* ointment. Right now, I want to take another look at your eyes."

I opened my eyes wide, and Grandfather leaned over me, his peculiar smell filling my nostrils.

"Very good," he said, leaning back. "I see no broken blood vessels, and no signs of concussion. I was afraid you might have been dropped on your head after you passed out. You will feel dizzy for a few hours, but after that you should be fine. I will make you some ginseng soup. It will help you feel better."

"Thank you," I said. "How long have you been conscious?"

"Not long. I was awakened by the sound of an outboard motor."

"They must have come on the river."

Grandfather nodded. "I am very grateful they did not harm you. It seems they only took what they came for."

"What was that?"

Grandfather didn't reply.

I thought about his antique Chinese armoire. There was a secret panel at the back in which he hid all of his most important things. He had shown me the contents once, and I remembered a few pieces of gold jewelry, some old photographs, and a couple of faded scrolls that

Grandfather refused to show me. Slim had been chopping at the armoire with the ax.

"They took your scrolls?" I asked.

"Scrolls?" Grandfather said; then he shook his head slowly. "No. They are of no consequence."

"Then why are you so upset? What did they take from your armoire?"

"Nothing. What they took was hidden in plain sight."

"I don't understand."

Grandfather looked me in the eye, and his face filled with sadness.

"Phoenix, they took my dragon bone."

I was confused. It didn't seem like such a big deal to me. Grandfather normally kept the dragon bone in an ornate porcelain container alongside his other Chinese herbs in a cupboard over the sink. The substance was a grayish white powder, and he put a minuscule amount of it into his tea every morning. He consumed lots of different herbs every day. He had them shipped to him from China by an old apothecary friend he called Paw-Paw. She had come to visit us once, and she regularly shipped him things like peony flower root, which was good for blood circulation; *Astragalus*, which was good for digestion; and wolfberries, which contain large amounts of natural antioxidants. Grandfather taught me about all the things he ate, and he even made me eat some of them sometimes. However, he never said a word about dragon bone.

I looked up dragon bone on the Internet, though, and found that it is technically a mineral, not an herb. It's basically fossilized animal bones that have been cooked and ground into powder. Grandfather's powder looked a little different from the pictures I saw on the Internet, but not much. His was more gray.

The descriptions said that dragon bone is high in calcium and potassium, and that it's often used as a calming agent. Apparently, it helps lower a person's heart rate. It's good for people who suffer from high blood pressure. People with insomnia use it, too. I figured Grandfather was embarrassed that he took it, which is why he never talked about it or explained the mineral's uses to me.

"I do know a little bit about dragon bone," I confessed. "It's pretty common on the Internet. Can't you just order more?"

Grandfather looked disgusted. "Calling that stuff you can buy on the Internet dragon bone is like calling a Pekingese puppy a Mongolian wolf. It is made from the bones of common animals. My dragon bone was made from the bones of actual dragons."

"You mean, dragons really existed?"

"Of course they did. As did dinosaurs and any number of currently extinct creatures. Is it really that difficult to believe?"

"I guess not," I said. "What makes real dragon bone so special compared with the other kind?"

"While modern dragon bone does have some legitimate uses, true dragon bone has different properties and provides enhanced . . . results."

"Like what?"

"I cannot tell you."

"Why not?"

Grandfather said nothing.

I frowned, knowing there was no point in pressing the issue. "Can't PawPaw ship you more?"

"There is no more."

"Well, can't you just eat more of something else? Wolfberries, maybe?"

"No."

"Is there someone else who can get you more?"

His eyes darkened. "I told you, there *is* no more."

I sat up, fighting another round of dizziness. Grandfather had never used that tone of voice before.

He must have seen the fear and confusion on my face. His voice softened. "I am sorry, Phoenix. I never expected this to happen. Not here in the United States, at least. True dragon bone is special. *Very* few people have heard of it, and until now I thought only three people in the world knew that it really existed."

"What does it do?"

He shook his head. "I cannot tell you."

"Why not?"

"Are you questioning my judgment?"

I considered saying yes, but then thought better of it. The last time I crossed him, my daily kung fu training sessions were so intense that it even hurt to sleep. I decided to change the subject.

"I'll call the police," I said.

"No police," Grandfather snapped.

I was dumbfounded. "I don't mean to be disrespectful, but we have to report this. They destroyed our home and almost killed us!"

"We do not have to do anything of the sort. This is my business. I will handle it."

"But—"

"Phoenix, I understand that you are only trying to be helpful, but I cannot risk any more people learning about dragon bone. I am upset enough that you know about it. If you were not such a trustworthy person, I would never have told you what it was called in the first place. I would have made up some other name for it. You have not mentioned dragon bone to anyone else, have you?"

"Never. I remember you told me to keep it secret, even though you never told me why."

"Good. Keeping it above the window was a mistake. All someone had to do was watch me from the trees and they would see me mixing it into my morning tea. Foolish. I let my guard down."

"It happens. Believe me, I know."

Grandfather shrugged. "I never expected someone in America to know about dragon bone. I also never expected to encounter someone here with such skills."

"What do you mean?" I asked.

"The man who grabbed me knew what he was doing. He had kung fu training. Only one other person has ever been able to immobilize me like that. His name was Fu. But that was a long, long time ago."

"His name was 'Tiger'? Was he in your kung fu class or something?"

"He was my temple brother."

I wasn't sure I had heard him right. "You lived in a *temple*?"

Grandfather nodded.

"Tell me about it!"

"No."

"Come on. I don't know anything about your past. You said once that you learned kung fu at a martial arts school."

"I did. It also happened to be my home. Think of it as a boarding school."

"I don't believe this. How long did you live there?"

"Nearly thirteen years."

"Why did you leave?"

"The temple was destroyed."

"What happened? An earthquake?"

Grandfather shook his head. "An attack led by one of my former brothers."

"Your temple was attacked? By your own temple brother? This sounds like a kung fu movie! Tell me more."

"It is a long story."

"I'm not going anywhere."

Grandfather groaned. "I am in an awkward position, Phoenix. You do deserve information. However, I am reluctant to tell anyone about my life in China, particularly my childhood, and especially about dragon bone. Even you would think me *chi seen*."

"*Chi seen?* Doesn't that mean 'crazy' in Cantonese?"

Grandfather nodded.

"Whatever it is, your past has caught up with you. You

have to tell me what is going on. Those guys wrecked our house. They sabotaged my bike so I would end up in the hospital. One of them even choked me unconscious. What are they going to do next, kill me?"

"Do not speak of such things."

"Why, because it just might happen?"

Grandfather stood and lowered his voice. "Someone is going to die, Phoenix, only it will not be you. They took my dragon bone."

I felt the color drain from my face.

"That is right," he said. "Now you know why I am so upset. I have only a few weeks to live."

7

I sat on my bed, staring at my grandfather. For the first time in my life, I wasn't sure I wanted to know about his past. He was going to die because he stopped putting powder into his tea?

I took a deep breath. "Are you sure about this?"

"I am sorry," Grandfather replied.

My mind began to race. Someone had to be able to help. I thought about my uncle, the doctor. He was my mother's brother, and he ran a nursing home in Indianapolis. Grandfather went there a couple of days a week to teach the residents a form of slow-motion Chinese exercise called tai chi.

"What about Uncle Tí?" I asked. "Isn't it his job to help people live longer?"

"I am sorry, Phoenix," Grandfather repeated. "No one can help me. As I have already told you, there is no more dragon bone."

"There has to be something we can do. I can't lose you. You and Uncle Tí are the only relatives I have left." I felt tears begin to pool in my eyes, but I was angry.

"You have to be strong."

"I *am* strong!" I shouted. "So are you! Why don't we fight back? What if we found the men who took it?"

"How might we do that?"

"I don't know! Think of something. You're old and wise."

Grandfather smiled. "I have thought about this longer than any person should have to. Believe me. Running out of dragon bone was inevitable. It simply happened a few years sooner than I thought."

I couldn't believe it. I wasn't done arguing. "Since it's gone, can't you at least tell me what true dragon bone does?"

Grandfather shook his head. "Its properties are the biggest secret of all. If I tell you what it does, I might as well tell you everything else."

"Please, Grandfather." The tears in my eyes began to fall, and I noticed Grandfather stiffen. He looked away.

"Right now," Grandfather said, "I do not know whom to suspect. I do not want to put you at any more risk by telling you too much."

"I can't possibly be at any more risk," I said. "Please, let me help you."

He sighed and turned back to me. "I do not know. Perhaps you could be of assistance. Since you have no knowledge of the past, you might form conclusions that elude me, and we might find a way to get it back. Maybe I *should* tell you its secrets."

I wiped the angry tears from my face. "Tell me."

"If I do, you must promise to never discuss this with anyone."

"I promise."

Grandfather nodded. "Very well. True dragon bone has the power to accelerate the body's healing processes, and it has been known to repair internal damage that is normally irreversible."

"What do you mean?"

"I know firsthand of a boy who lost his eyesight, but after taking dragon bone, his vision returned."

"Really? How come more people don't know about it?"

"The properties of true dragon bone used to be fairly well known, but it was scarce. And expensive. A time came when a few people stockpiled every bit they could. These stockpiles were soon depleted, and no one could find any more dragon bones. Eventually, apothecaries began to use fossilized bones from different animals, which provided some similar health benefits—helping people sleep, for instance. They soon forgot about the other properties of real dragon bone."

"They forgot?"

"People forget all sorts of things, Phoenix, especially when it comes to medicinal herbs."

"So you were one of the people who stockpiled it?"

"Yes."

This was sounding a little far-fetched, but Grandfather had never lied before. "Why did you keep the dragon bone to yourselves? I mean, couldn't it be used to help others?"

"Yes, but we found that it had effects beyond the acceleration of general healing. Most notably, it prolonged people's lives. We did not want it to fall into the wrong hands."

"I don't understand."

"A dishonorable person who lives a very long time could amass a huge fortune and, in turn, become extremely powerful. That power could be put to ill use."

"But you aren't rich."

"No."

"Then why did you and others keep taking it?"

"I suppose we were greedy in other ways."

"How?"

"We did not want it to end."

"Didn't want what to end?"

"Our lives," Grandfather said. "At least, that has been my motivation. While I have no fortune to speak of in monetary terms, I have you. You are the reason I continue. Before you, there were others who needed me. It seems there has always been someone in need of my help. I suppose I am also selfish. I enjoy life too much to leave it."

I didn't know what to say. This really was *chi seen*. "Are you sure you'll die if you stop taking it?"

"Unfortunately, yes. I know two people who stopped, and they passed away within one lunar cycle—a month. There was a third who stopped, but he eventually started taking it again. In the end, he died of other causes. Dragon bone does not make you immortal. If a person is injured and the wound is too great, no amount of dragon bone will help." ·

"So you take it once, and you're addicted for life?"

"No. It is not an addiction. It is more like a codependency. It feeds you, but you also feed it."

"Like a parasite that gives something back to its host?" I asked. "We learned about that in school. It's called a symbiotic relationship."

"Exactly. In this case, it is a bond that must be closely monitored. If a person consumes dragon bone recklessly, it can become one with his or her system. The connection may be too strong to break. Skilled apothecaries knew to administer only the tiniest amounts, and to allow patients to take it for only a few days. Even then, some patients underwent a period of extended lethargy once they stopped consuming it. They were utterly exhausted, unable to even get out of bed."

"Isn't there some kind of antidote?"

"No. However, as I have said, if a person is not reckless with it, they can sever the bond. They can also fight the lethargy with extreme physical exertion, shortening the recovery period. It seems that sweating helps to disconnect the dragon bone's hold and purge it from one's system."

I thought about Grandfather's peculiar scent whenever he exerted himself. "There is dragon bone in *your* sweat, isn't there?"

He nodded.

"Who were the dragon bone users who died, and why did they stop taking it?"

"One was an old apothecary named LoBak from the city of Hangzhou in southeastern China. He was a good man. After his granddaughter died in childbirth, he decided that he had seen enough death for one lifetime. The other was HukJee—'Black Pig'—a black market dealer from the more northern city of Jinan. HukJee and LoBak were best friends. HukJee decided that he, too, had had enough of what the world had to offer. He had no desire to continue on without his best friend. The two of them distributed their remaining dragon bone supplies to the rest of us, and they passed away together. If anyone could have been able to locate more dragon bone, it was HukJee. But he never could. He tried for more years than you could believe, just for the fun of looking for it."

"Wow," I said. "What about the third person?"

"The one who stopped and started again, but died anyway, was another of my temple brothers. His name was Ying, or 'Eagle.' He was the first person I ever knew to use the substance. He began taking it at age sixteen in an effort to strengthen the Dragon spirit that lived inside him. He used to mix his dragon bone with fresh snake blood to make it even more potent, but he eventually decided that he was enough of a Dragon without the dragon bone, and he stopped consuming it. I later learned that he had to start taking it again because of the lethargy. In the end, he died of a sword wound that was too great for any amount of dragon bone to overcome."

"So you can't just stop taking it and lie around until your energy returns?"

"Me specifically? No. Over time, I have taken less and less and can still function normally. Even so, there is a minimum amount that I require, and I have been at that minimum for more years than I can count. When someone as old as I am takes it for as long as I have, just as LoBak and HukJee did, the energy does not return. It leaves with the dragon bone, and your life goes with it."

"How long have you been taking it?"

"I would rather not say."

"Please, Grandfather. No more secrets."

Grandfather's brow furrowed. "Some things should not be shared. This piece of information would change our relationship. I do not want that."

"Knowing your age won't change a thing," I said. "Some people live to be a hundred and fifteen years old or more these days. That's like four generations. So, what are you, one-thirty? One-fifty?"

Grandfather didn't answer.

"Wait a minute," I said. "I know what you're worried about. You're not really my grandfather, are you? You're actually my great-grandfather or maybe my great-great-grandfather. Right?"

Grandfather nodded.

"Whew! That is strange, but I can accept it."

"Can you? Think about it for a moment."

I did, and Grandfather was right. This changed everything I thought I knew about my family. However, I still wanted answers. "What happened to my actual grand-father, my mother's father?"

"He died of lung cancer in China, as did his wife, your grandmother. They both smoked."

I frowned. That did hurt to hear. But I wanted more. "What about Uncle Tí? Is he really my uncle?"

"Yes. He was your mother's older brother—her only sibling."

"Does he know about any of this?"

"He has his hunches about my true age, but we have never discussed it openly. He once did a complete phys-ical examination of me and asked for a sample of the herbs I take, but I refused to give him any of my dragon bone."

"What about my father's parents from Indiana? I re-member you telling me once that they both died of heart attacks."

"They did, and your father did not have any siblings or extended family members, either. Your uncle and I are the only family you have left. I am sorry."

I shrugged.

"What are you feeling, Phoenix? Be honest."

I paused, then swallowed hard. "I'll be fine. You had your reasons for pretending to be my grandfather, and in every important way you are. You're my mother and fa-ther, too. I can still call you Grandfather, can't I?"

I saw tears welling in his eyes. "I would be honored if you did," he said.

I didn't know what to say. I'd never seen him tear up before.

He saw that I was concerned. "Do not worry. I am simply moved by your words. I now believe I must answer your original question completely and honestly. I do not know how you will react, but I feel it is important. According to the Western calendar, I was born in the year 1638."

I choked out loud, and my brain skipped as I did the math. "You mean you're more than three hundred and seventy years old?"

"Yes."

"That's . . . unbelievable."

Grandfather folded his arms. "Is it? Tortoises live nearly two hundred years. Koi fish live two hundred and thirty. Greenland sharks may live three or even four hundred years. There is a pine tree in Sweden that is nearly ten thousand years old. The list goes on."

"But you are a *person*. I mean—you still are a person, right?"

Grandfather smirked. "I would hope so."

I took a deep breath. "Well, *I* know who and what you are. You are my grandfather, and I want you around. There are stories from all over the world about people living for hundreds of years in the old days. Maybe those people knew about dragon bone, too. I want to help you."

"You are a good boy, Phoenix. You make me proud."

"Let's see how good I really am," I said. "We need to think of a plan. You said that LoBak, HukJee, Ying, and you used dragon bone. Are there any others?"

"Two. That I know of."

"Are they still alive?"

"Yes. Both."

I felt a glimmer of hope. "Can't you get more from them?"

"Even if the others were willing to share, I would not accept it. Every day they give me is one day less for them."

"I'll ask them, then. Grandfather, I *need* you. While Uncle Tí is nice enough, I want you with me."

He looked away again.

I wasn't about to give up. I snapped my fingers. "Paw-Paw is one, isn't she? Even you call her Grandmother. *PawPaw* means 'Grandmother' in Mandarin Chinese, right?"

Grandfather grimaced. "She is indeed, but I forbid you to ask her. I know how much she has left. It is not enough. Her reason for remaining among the living is far less selfish than mine. She runs a free clinic to treat sick people who have no money. Without her, hundreds would die each year. Perhaps thousands."

"But—"

"No!" Grandfather said firmly. He turned back to face me.

I pounded my fist against my thigh. "I have never disobeyed you, Grandfather, but I will not sit back and watch you die. I'm going to call her. You will not stop me."

Grandfather's eyes narrowed, and so did mine. We locked eyes like bulls locking horns. I had been staring down competitors at my mountain bike races for years. No one could hold up to my intense green eyes.

Grandfather blinked. "You are stubborn."

"I got it from you," I mumbled.

Grandfather's face darkened, but his anger soon gave way to a faint smile. "Fine," he said. "You win."

I felt my heart skip a beat. "What did you just say?"

"I said, *you win.* I will arrange for you to see PawPaw, but I ask you not to take any of her dragon bone. You could, however, approach the other person I have alluded to. PawPaw can help you find him. I do not always see eye to eye with this man, and he and I have not spoken directly in many, many years. He is yet another of my temple brothers, but we had a falling out. I would never ask him for a favor such as this, but you seem determined to take action, so I will let you try, for both our sakes. It will take some effort to reach him, but you are young and strong. I have faith you will succeed. While I am strong at this moment, my health will deteriorate quickly. You will have to go alone. You have a good heart. I believe that if he meets you, he will be willing to share a sufficient quantity of dragon bone for me to live long enough to see you grow into a man."

I grinned. "That sounds good to me."

"If you are to do this," Grandfather said, "time is of the essence. PawPaw currently lives in Beijing, which is twelve hours ahead of us this time of year. She is asleep now, but she is an early riser. We shall call her tonight, when it will be morning for her."

"What are we going to do in the meantime?"

"You will continue to rest. This afternoon, I have a tai chi class to teach at the nursing home. You will come with me. After class, we will talk with your uncle. Perhaps he can accelerate the processing of your international travel documentation by declaring your trip a medical emergency on my behalf. You should leave as soon as possible."

"So I'm really going to China?"

Grandfather nodded.

"Woo-hoo! I won't let you down, Grandfather. That's a promise."

STAGE TWO

SECOND RULE OF CYCLING
Change Gears Early and Often

8

Forty-eight hours later, I found myself on an airplane departing New York and bound for Beijing. I could hardly believe it. It was Asian Airlines flight 333—triple lucky. I did indeed feel fortunate. I was going to save Grandfather.

We'd spent the past two days straightening up the mess Slim and Meathead had made, plus making plans for my trip. My uncle Tí had come through for us in more ways than one. He took one look at Grandfather and knew something wasn't quite right with him. A quick check of Grandfather's pulse, and Uncle Tí demanded the whole story. Grandfather was reluctant at first, but in the end he told my uncle everything, including what he knew about dragon bone.

I expected Uncle Tí to be angry, considering Grandfather had kept such significant secrets from him for so long. But it turned out he was more sad than anything else, mostly because of what Grandfather's situation and condition meant for me. Once all of Uncle Tí's questions were answered, he announced that he had a secret of his own. Years ago, when Grandfather had denied him a sample of dragon bone, Uncle Tí took some anyway. It seemed he was just as sneaky as Grandfather.

My uncle had run tests on the substance, but he found that the more tests he ran, the more questions arose. He eventually gave up, classifying dragon bone in his own mind as some type of dormant bacteria or virus that woke up when introduced to a host and fused itself to the host's living cells. The longer the exposure, the stronger the fusion. He was opposed to testing anything on live animals, so his experiments had been on individual cells only. He had no idea how a complex living creature would be affected by the cellular changes. Thanks to Grandfather's explanations, he now knew, and he wasn't happy about it. In fact, he was incredibly disappointed with Grandfather. To Uncle Tí, doing anything to disrupt the natural cycle of life and death was taboo.

Despite his personal views, my uncle agreed to help, going so far as to present Grandfather with a surprise— a small supply of dragon bone that he had never tested. He'd saved it all these years. It wasn't much, but it would last Grandfather about a week. While Grandfather was angry that Uncle Tí had stolen from him, he was also grateful. I was, too.

My uncle helped us in other ways. He not only paid for my flight to China, he helped Grandfather take care of all my paperwork. I had no idea that there was so much necessary for a person to travel internationally.

THE FIVE ANCESTORS OUT OF THE ASHES

While I had never traveled outside the United States, I did have a current passport. A travel visa, however, was a different matter. Especially a visa that needed to be rush-issued for a minor traveling solo to China. Uncle Tí grudgingly prepared documents to classify my trip as an immediate medical necessity and forwarded them along with a visa request to the Chinese consulate-general in Chicago. It worked. I was overnighted a short-term travel visa.

Most important of all, Uncle Tí said he would keep an eye on Grandfather while I was gone. He would even take Grandfather to the nursing home if Grandfather's condition should merit it. That helped set my mind a bit more at ease.

As for my trip, I flew from Indianapolis to New York, and now I was really on my way to China. Once I arrived, PawPaw would take care of everything, beginning with meeting me at the Beijing airport customs area. If I had not been a minor, she would have had to wait for me all the way down in baggage claim. I hadn't seen her in years, but she had assured me over the phone that she would recognize me. Apparently, there weren't many thirteen-year-old half-Chinese boys with reddish-brown hair, freckles, and green eyes in Beijing. As I remembered, PawPaw was a very nice lady. Best of all, she spoke English perfectly.

I did speak some Mandarin Chinese, the dialect spoken in Beijing and throughout most of China. I also knew a few words in Cantonese, because Grandfather spoke that as well. However, my vocabulary was limited mostly to kung fu terms and the names of appendages and internal organs most likely to be damaged while practicing martial arts. For example, I knew how to say things like "Please stop, Grandfather, you're breaking my arm," and "Uh-oh, I believe your Crane Kick has ruptured my spleen." These phrases were useful during training sessions, but not very helpful in everyday conversation.

I had a translation dictionary with me, but it was next to useless because Chinese is a tonal language, and like most people, I have difficulty deciphering all the special marks used to identify the language's numerous rising and falling tones. I was more than a little worried.

Hopefully, the man I was supposed to locate in China spoke English. Grandfather didn't know if he did. In fact, Grandfather said very little about the man, other than mentioning that they had been temple brothers, which meant that the man, like Grandfather, had to be very old. Grandfather wouldn't even tell me his name, commenting that the man made a habit of changing his name so often, Grandfather had no idea what to call him. It was clear that Grandfather did not like him very much.

The last Grandfather had heard, this mystery man lived at the ruins of the temple where Grandfather grew up. It was called Cangzhen Temple, which Grandfather said meant "Hidden Truth Temple." When I asked what sort of truth was hidden at the temple, Grandfather replied that I should ask the mystery man. I couldn't imagine what might have happened between this person and Grandfather, but I hoped to find out. Perhaps the man might be willing to shed some light on the past that Grandfather preferred to keep secret.

As for my own secrets, it seemed I was now keeping several, and I didn't like it one bit. Jake had called a couple of times to see how I was doing after being knocked out during the race, and each time we spoke, I found myself holding back more and more information. It was frustrating. I told him I was going to China, of course, but all I said was that I was going there on family business and Grandfather had asked me not to talk about it. I promised him I would tell him more when I got back. Fortunately, Jake knew how Grandfather was about secrets, so he understood.

Jake and I also talked about Ryan. Jake's dad had spoken with Ryan's mom at the race, and she had been as surprised as everyone else by Ryan's mental and physical transformation when he returned from Belgium. According to his mom, Ryan didn't make any friends over there, so he spent nearly all of his free time in the Team Vanderhausen weight room. As for his mean streak and tantrum in the parking lot, she said he had been fine all week until they arrived at the race. Right before the start, she noticed him prepping alone, glaring at Jake and me as we cracked jokes. She knew he was jealous of what good friends Jake and I were, and how well we rode. Ryan had told her these things as far back as the funeral in November. In fact, a big part of the reason he went to Belgium in January was because kids in our hometown had stopped talking to him. As strange as it may sound, I kind of felt sorry for him.

The airplane began to bank gently to one side, and I lowered my window shade, blocking out the blinding morning sun. I needed a break from thinking about all the things that had happened over the past few days, and what I might encounter in the coming week. I turned on the overhead reading light and grabbed one of the adventure novels I'd brought, then eased my seat back and settled in for the thirteen-and-a-half-hour flight to Beijing International Airport.

9

Thanks to minimal headwinds, I landed in Beijing half an hour ahead of schedule. Between the thirteen-hour flight and the twelve-hour time difference, I arrived twenty-five hours after I'd left. It was ten a.m. in Beijing, but my body thought it was ten p.m. the previous night. I sort of wished I'd gotten a few hours of sleep on the plane. The book I'd been reading had been too good to put down.

We taxied up to the terminal, and I stepped out into a different world. While the airports in the United States had been crowded, this place was pure mayhem. Thousands of arriving passengers were being corralled like cattle and funneled through mazes of roped partitions leading into the customs area. Everyone was in a hurry, and nearly everyone was smoking. The humid air stank of cigarettes, and a yellow fog hung near the ceiling, obscuring many of the signs. The signs were in Chinese and English, but I still had no idea which line I was supposed to get into. This place was insane. There was no way PawPaw was going to find me.

As I stood trying to get my bearings in the nicotine haze, someone with a heavy Chinese accent made an announcement in English over the airport's loudspeakers, but I didn't catch what it was. The man behind me motioned to a lane that was opening up. "This way, mate," he said in a cool Australian accent. "Aussies, Americans, and Canadians. I reckon you're one of the above, like me."

"Right," I replied. "Thanks. You go first. I've never done this before."

The man nodded and stepped around me. I followed him toward a series of tall booths fronted with thick glass. There were lanes between the booths, and standing just inside the newly opened lane was an old Chinese woman with thinning white hair offset by shockingly clear eyes that seemed to peer into my very essence. She wore a jogging suit and bright white Converse high-tops with pink laces tied all the way up her ankles. While I didn't recognize her face, I remembered those eyes. I also remembered that Grandfather often sent PawPaw American clothing. It had to be her.

I waved, and PawPaw smiled, waving back. I felt a flood of relief. I waited for my turn; then I stepped up to a booth and pulled out my passport and other documents. The official flipped through my papers with hands clad in blue surgical gloves. He stamped my passport and handed everything back, then waved me off.

I slipped through the lane and headed for PawPaw. She greeted me in English.

"Phoenix!" she said. "It is such a pleasure to see you again! You've grown so much. And you're so handsome! It is fortunate that you look little like your grandfather. He is a wonderful man, but his face is too long and he always looks as though he just swallowed something sour."

I smiled. "It's great to see you again, too, PawPaw. I should call you that, right?"

"Of course," she replied, her smile broadening. She leaned close and lowered her voice. "People have been calling me that for generations." She winked.

I nodded. Judging from the extraordinarily deep laugh lines in her face, it was easy to believe that she had been around a few hundred years, grinning the entire time.

PawPaw began to walk, her voice returning to normal volume. "We have one more customs checkpoint to go through; then we can collect your baggage and get out of here. We might even be able to get you onto an earlier coach."

"Coach?" I asked, following her through the throngs of travelers.

"A bus," she replied. "You're going to the city of Kaifeng."

Before I could ask more, she stopped at a long row of low tables. Behind each table was another customs official. I saw travelers opening their carry-on bags for the officials. Some travelers were told to dump the entire contents onto the tables. I waited for my turn, stepped up to a table, and unzipped my duffel bag. The official looked at me, then at PawPaw, and waved us on without bothering to go through the bag. PawPaw seemed pleased. She began to weave her way through the crowds again.

"That was quick," she said. "This is good. By catching the earlier bus, you will arrive in Kaifeng before dark. That will make me feel better. There are worse places you could be in China than Kaifeng after dark, but not many."

I was confused. "I thought I was going to spend at least one night in Beijing with you."

"Heavens, no! You have work to do. Your body is probably telling you that it is time to go to sleep, but you can sleep on the ride south. Your bus trip will take nine or ten hours, depending on how many farm animals you encounter wandering across the roads. You could be delayed by flocks of sheep or whole herds of cattle. Outside the big cities, China is quite rural."

I felt a pang of nervousness in my gut.

"Don't worry," PawPaw said in a cheery voice. "I would never send you out alone without ammunition." She patted one of her pockets. "I will show you this later. For now, let us talk of other things. Do you have any questions?"

"Tons," I said. "Where do I go after Kaifeng?"

"You will ultimately travel about sixty miles farther, deep into Henan Province."

"That's south, right?"

"Yes, and it is going to be hot. Beijing is about the

same latitude as your home near Indianapolis, so you can expect roughly the same weather here. Where you are headed will be even hotter."

I gave her a quizzical look.

"I am addicted to Internet satellite map software," PawPaw admitted with a chuckle. "I love researching medicinal herbs and the places they grow around the world."

"I see," I said. Grandfather didn't even know how to turn on a computer.

We reached baggage claim, and I couldn't believe how many luggage carousels were snaking in and out of the walls. PawPaw scanned a series of information monitors and pointed across the expansive area. "This way."

We reached the conveyor belt assigned for my flight, and I grabbed the medium-sized camping backpack that Grandfather had bought for me. It was gliding between an expensive-looking black leather suitcase and a torn cardboard box bound with twine and duct tape. I found it funny that everyone's luggage traveled the same way, regardless of how much a person had spent on it. I grabbed my pack and shoved my duffel into it. Then I slung the pack onto my shoulders and headed for the exit with PawPaw.

Once we were outside, I felt a warm breeze hit my face. I inhaled deeply, which sent me into a coughing fit. The smog outside was nearly as bad as the cigarette smoke inside.

"The air quality is much better beyond the city,"

PawPaw said. "Fewer people can afford cars out there. Excessive vehicle exhaust is the price we pay in the cities for a booming economy."

My coughing subsided, and I followed her to a line of taxicabs. We climbed into one, and she began to haggle with the driver. Part of the conversation concerned payment, but I had no idea what the rest was about.

We pulled away from the curb, and PawPaw turned to me. "Did you understand that?"

"A little," I replied. "Something about the cab fare."

"That's right. You'll get the hang of it. Just ask people to speak slowly, and don't be afraid to ask them to repeat themselves. Whenever you are about to purchase something, regardless of the situation or store, always push for a lower price, especially in the small towns and villages."

My eyebrows rose. "Villages?"

"Beyond Kaifeng, you will have to travel on foot. You will pass through a few villages. You can buy food there, along with any other supplies you might need."

"How am I supposed to find my way around? I don't think my Chinese is good enough to ask directions."

PawPaw removed a palm-sized electronic device from her jacket pocket. She handed it to me.

"What is this?" I asked.

"Your ammunition," she replied. "A GPS unit. I've programmed the route I think you should take."

I glanced at the cab driver. He didn't appear to be following our conversation in English, but I lowered my voice, just in case. "You have the GPS coordinates of a long-forgotten temple?"

"Not exactly," PawPaw said, "but the destination I have input is certainly close. You will find it in the 'trails' section. I've also downloaded city maps and transportation schedules into the unit so you will know where to go once you get off the bus. There is even a lodging function where you can find hotels."

I suddenly felt a lot better. "Thank you so much! I can't believe you did all of this."

"Why, because I'm old? Ha! I love technology, especially the Internet. Purchasing that GPS unit was the best thing I've done in years. It gave me an excuse to buy a new notebook computer. My old one didn't have the right ports to connect to the GPS. You can return the GPS to me when you're through. I would have gotten you a pay-as-you-go cell phone, but there is no service where you are going."

"I don't know what to say."

"You don't have to say anything, Phoenix. We are nearly there, anyway. Look."

I glanced through the windshield and saw that we were coming up to a gigantic bus terminal.

"I realize that traveling alone at your age must seem strange to you," PawPaw said, "but do not fear. You will see many young people your age and even younger getting on these long-distance buses without adult companions. Some of them are traveling to stay with distant family members, while others have completed the eighth grade and have quit school in their villages to find work in the cities to help support their parents and siblings. This has been going on for thousands of years."

"I understand," I said. "Grandfather told me all about it."

"Very good."

We reached the bus terminal drop-off point, and the taxi pulled over. PawPaw leaned forward to pay the driver, and for the first time since leaving the smoke-filled airport, I noticed the unmistakable scent hovering around her. She smelled just like Grandfather.

PawPaw climbed out of the cab and began to push her way toward a busy counter protruding from the side of the building. I grabbed my pack and followed. Five minutes later, I was holding a round-trip bus ticket to Kaifeng.

"The return voucher is valid for one week," PawPaw said. "That should be plenty of time. Find a nice hotel in Kaifeng before the sun sets tonight, and stay off the streets. People will want to talk with you because of your unique appearance, but do not indulge them, regardless of the time of day. Most strangers will be harmless, but there are some questionable characters out there, especially in Kaifeng. Sometime I will have to tell you about an inn called the Jade Phoenix that used to be there. I imagine your grandfather has never mentioned it."

"No, he hasn't," I said. "Is that where my name comes from?"

PawPaw thought a moment. "You know, that's a very good question. I never made the connection. I'll have to remember to ask your grandfather, though only the heavens know if he'll give me an answer." She patted me on the shoulder. "Go to bed early tonight, and wake with the rising sun. You have to make haste, for your stubborn, secretive grandfather's sake."

I began to thank her, but PawPaw gave me a shove in the direction of a nearby bus idling in the street. People were boarding it.

"There is no need for thank-yous and no time for goodbyes," she said. "That is your bus and it is about to leave. I will call your grandfather to let him know that you arrived safely." She threw a granola bar at me, and I caught it. "Sorry I don't have any more food for you. I will cook you a huge meal the next time we meet. You will see me again soon enough."

I nodded and hurried toward the bus, unaware of just how wrong PawPaw was.

10

An hour outside Beijing's high-rises and crowded streets, the road beyond my bus window looked strangely familiar. Soybean farms dotted the landscape, and cows, sheep, and chickens milled about fenced fields. If it weren't for the farmers sporting large straw hats instead of John Deere baseball caps, I would have sworn I was back home in the American Midwest.

Even the bus itself felt American. I'd once taken a Greyhound bus to Chicago's Chinatown with Grandfather, and this one looked exactly the same, right down to the worn seats. As I had on my flight over, I cranked my seat back, only this time the steady hum of the road and the bus's gentle rocking motion eventually coaxed me to sleep.

I woke with a start hours later to find that we'd reached the end of the line. I checked my watch. I'd slept almost the entire day. I wiped the sleep from my eyes and looked over my pack. It appeared to be just as I'd left it. Nobody's fingers had found their way in. Even the GPS unit was still in the side pocket. I was good to go.

I scarfed down the granola bar PawPaw had given me and climbed off the bus with the other passengers—all of them Chinese. I saw that we were inside some kind of garage, surrounded by more buses. The air was thick with exhaust, and the ground was slick with oil. I noticed a door with daylight beyond and headed for it.

I stepped outside, into the evening sun. It wouldn't be dark for a couple more hours, but I decided to take PawPaw's advice and find a hotel right away. I also needed to find some more food.

I headed down the main street outside the bus terminal, looking for a restaurant, and quickly lost my appetite. The city, or at least this section of it, looked like a war zone. The buildings here were crumbling, and the streets were overflowing with trash. I imagined shady individuals watching my every move from the numerous dark alleyways. I wanted to pull out the GPS unit and try to find a nicer section of town, but I was worried that someone would dart out from the shadows and steal the GPS.

I decided to head back to the bus terminal, when I heard a noise behind me. I tried to turn around, but couldn't. Someone had grabbed my backpack.

I lunged forward, trying to break out of the person's grip, and the pack's straps slipped from my shoulders. I bent my elbows, barely catching the straps in time. I continued driving my body away from the thief, but it was no use. Whoever it was was too strong. In fact, he was slowly pulling me toward him.

I heard a high-pitched laugh, and I glanced over my shoulder to see a Chinese kid about sixteen years old. His face was lean, and he had wild, beady eyes. His feet were set roughly shoulder-width apart, and his knees were bent in a deep Horse Stance, anchoring him solidly to the ground. He felt stronger than I was and based on that stance, there was a good chance he knew kung fu. Which meant that if I wanted to keep my pack, I was going to have to either be quicker than he was, or fight dirty.

Or both.

I lunged backward, shifting my hips closer to his. At the same time, I swept my right leg up and back in a powerful arc, like a scorpion raising its stinger. The bottom of my hiking boot connected with the kid's groin, and he let out a piercing shriek. He let go of my pack, and I felt his hands grab at the hair on the back of my head.

I pivoted to my right and released my left arm from my pack sling. I swung the pack around, batting away his hands, but he rushed toward me. My left arm was already cocked behind me, and as he closed the gap, I swung an overhand left fist at his face. He saw it coming and turned his head, and my punch clipped him behind the ear.

He stopped short, his legs turning to Jell-O. I saw a fog settle over his eyes. However, he managed to stay on his feet. He was tough.

He also wasn't stupid. He knew when to quit. He turned and ran off in an odd, loping stride.

I glanced around, but saw no one else coming at me.

I looked down at my hands and realized that they were trembling, probably from the adrenaline burst that had fueled my Scorpion Kick. While I'd been studying kung fu forever, that was the first time I'd ever had to use it in real life. It was nothing like I'd imagined. I didn't like it. The knuckles on my left hand were sore, and my ears were ringing, also because of the adrenaline.

I took another look around, trying to calm my jittery nerves before heading back to the bus terminal, and a sign jutting out from the side of a dilapidated building farther down the road caught my attention. I couldn't decipher all the Chinese characters, but I did recognize one. It said BICYCLE.

It occurred to me that a few minutes inside a bike shop might help push the attack out of my mind. Besides, I'd never been inside a Chinese bike shop. It could be interesting.

I headed for the storefront, if it could be called that. The two-story building was in bad shape, its bricks crumbling into the cracked sidewalk. Large windows were boarded over with sheets of plywood. If it weren't for a second small sign, this one on the heavy metal front door, I would have headed back to the bus terminal without giving the building another thought. The small sign contained only one Chinese character, but I could read it. It said OPEN.

I gave the battered door a gentle tug, and to my surprise it swung outward smoothly on well-oiled hinges. I stepped inside and closed the door behind me. Looking around, I had to blink several times to make sure I wasn't imagining what I was seeing. It was one of the most amazing sights I'd ever encountered.

Before me was a sea of bicycles. There were mountain bikes, road bikes, and cyclocross bikes. There were tricycles, unicycles, and tandem bikes. There were BMX bikes, load-hauling bikes, and recumbent bikes. It was unbelievable.

Most astonishing of all was that the bikes were from every major manufacturer around the world. The shops back in the United States would kill for an inventory like this. American shops were tied to contracts with specific manufacturers, which meant they could carry only certain things from certain brands. This shop obviously had no such agreements.

Standing with my mouth agape, I heard a girl's voice ring out in English.

"Do you like?"

I closed my mouth and glanced about, but didn't see anyone. Then I heard movement behind a tall counter toward the back of the shop and saw a small, grease-covered individual appear from behind it. The person was wearing stained coveralls, black work boots, and a Detroit Tigers baseball cap pulled low. It didn't look like any girl I had ever seen before.

A small hand with gunk-clogged fingernails removed the hat, and a wave of shimmering sable hair spilled out. *Now* she looked like a girl.

"I said, 'Do you like?'" the girl asked again. "You speak English, yes?"

"Yes," I replied. "And I like."

She smiled. "What exactly do you like?"

I felt my face flush, and I waved a hand toward the rows of bicycles blanketing the shop floor. "I—I was talking about the bikes."

The girl pouted as she approached me. "Oh." She wiped grease from her palms with a dirty rag dangling from her back pocket and stuck out her hand. "My name is Tiě Hú Dié. Welcome to the finest bicycle shop in Henan Province."

Still embarrassed, I took her hand. It was small and warm, and holding it made me feel strange. I let go.

"I'm Phoenix Collins," I mumbled.

"Phoenix?"

"Yes."

"That is a girl's name."

I frowned. "Not according to my grandfather, and he's Chinese."

"But you're American, yes?"

I stared at her. "How did you know?"

"Your accent."

"Oh."

"So, Phoenix is your first name?" she asked.

I remembered that people from many Asian countries gave their last name first. "That's right," I said.

"Then you would say that my name is Hú Dié Tiě. You may call me Hú Dié."

She pronounced it "Hoo DEE-ay."

"Butterfly?" I asked.

"Correct," she said. "You speak Chinese?"

"*Yí dian dian,*" I replied. "A little. What does *Tiě* mean?"

She flashed a mischievous smile. "Guess."

"I have no idea."

"Come on, Phoenix, guess my name."

I fought the urge to laugh as the story of Rumpel-stiltskin popped into my head. Never one to back down from a challenge, I looked her over and swallowed a lump that was inexplicably forming in my throat. I figured I should guess something nice. I asked, "Does *Tiě* mean . . . 'lovely'?"

To my surprise, her smile disappeared, and she punched me in the arm. "No," she said. "Guess again."

I rubbed my arm. She was strong. "Um," I said, trying hard to think of a word that paired well with *butterfly*. "How about . . . 'delicate'?"

She punched me again, harder this time.

"Ouch!" I said. "That hurt. What's wrong with you?"

"What's wrong with me? What's wrong with *you*? Get punched by a girl, and you squirm like an eel. Guess again."

I shook my head. What was up with this girl? Was she flirting? Did she just want attention? Regardless, I wasn't interested. Girls were the last thing on my mind. "This is stupid," I said. "I give up."

"Quitter."

"I am *not* a quitter."

"Guess again, then."

I glared at her.

She glared back. "Would you like a clue?" she asked.

"Whatever."

She punched me a third time. This time I felt as if I'd been hit with a hammer.

I yelped and jumped backward. "Are you insane?"

Hú Dié giggled. "That was your clue." She pushed the sleeves of her coveralls up all the way to her shoulders and lifted both arms in a bodybuilder's pose. She flexed, displaying perfectly toned biceps and rock-hard triceps. *"Tiě,"* she said, "means 'iron.' I am Iron Butterfly."

I rubbed my arm again. "You are *Psycho* Butterfly."

"And you are an infant. Stop whining."

I'd had enough of her. I turned away and headed for the door.

"Wait!" she called out. "Please don't leave. I am only joking."

I kept walking.

"Please? Pretty, pretty please?"

I stopped. I looked back at her. "Why should I stay here and keep getting abused?"

"I promise I'll stop. I like talking with you. I'm sorry if I tease too much. It is just my way."

I glanced around at the bikes once more, and an idea began to form. Why in the world would I hike to this Cangzhen Temple when I could ride there? This shop had plenty of mountain bikes. Maybe I could afford to buy one? Better yet, maybe I could rent one. It would be a lot cheaper.

"I need to speak with the manager," I said.

"Huh?"

"The manager," I repeated. "The boss. The head honcho. Your leader. I need to speak with him."

She put her hands on her hips. "*I* am the manager. I am also the head mechanic, and the owner."

I looked at her in wonder. "This is all yours?"

"Yes. Technically, my father and I own it together, but I do all the work. He is usually busy with other things. This is my shop. Just ask him when he comes back later."

"How old are you?"

"Fourteen. How old are you?"

"Thirteen." I looked around. "How do you find time to manage all of this? Did you drop out of school or something?"

"Do I speak English like an intermediate school dropout?"

I felt my face beginning to flush again. "Um, no. Sorry."

"I'll take that as a compliment, then," she said. "I want to go to college in America or Australia one day, so I work very hard on my English. I even pay for a special tutor with my own money. I do not want to spend my whole life with grease underneath my fingernails, you know."

I nodded, a new respect growing for her. Maybe she wasn't psycho, after all—just feisty. "Do you rent bicycles?" I asked.

"For you? Possibly."

"What's that supposed to mean? '*Possibly.*'"

"It's just that we don't normally rent bicycles here. I rarely sell them to individuals, either. No one bothers to come to this section of Kaifeng unless they are going to the bus terminal. We are wholesalers. The bikes you see will be sent to bike shops across China."

"Oh," I said, my irritation quickly dissolving. "I was wondering how you could have so many different brands in one place. How much to rent one?"

"Pick a bike first; then we'll see if we can work something out."

I spotted a blue and white dual-suspension mountain bike and walked over to it. It was a beauty. I knelt down to examine the components and froze. "I hate to tell you this," I said, "but this bike is a copy."

"What do you mean?"

"It is not an original from the manufacturer. It was made by someone else."

"How do you know?"

I pointed to a joint where two sections of the frame came together. "See this weld? It wasn't done by the manufacturer. They use machines. This was done by hand. The weld probably won't hold up to hard riding."

"It will hold," she said in a defensive tone.

"How can you be so sure?"

"Because I welded it."

I jumped to my feet. "*You* built this bike?"

She nodded. "It is a very good reproduction, is it not? I even painted it. Look." She pointed behind the tall counter at the back of the shop.

I walked over to the counter and saw a small spray booth for painting beyond it. I also saw a large assortment of raw aluminum and steel tubing to be bent into bike frame sections, plus cutting torches, welding equipment, and numerous trays of wrenches, hammers, pliers, and other tools.

"Which of these bikes did you build?" I asked.

"All of them. I built the frames from scratch, then added the components."

"But there are like two hundred bikes here, and they are all different types!"

"There are currently two hundred twenty-one."

"Incredible," I said. "How much do they sell for?"

"Retail price, of course."

I wasn't sure that I had heard her right. "You mean people pay the same price for your copies as they would for the real thing? Don't you tell them that they are fakes?"

"My customers know that these are replicas. As for what they tell *their* customers, that is none of my business."

"But that's cheating."

"No. I am honest about the origin of my bikes."

I shook my head.

"Oh, come on," she said. "Bike companies copy each other's designs all the time, right down to the paint schemes. No one is stopping them from stealing my designs."

"What do you know about bike design?"

"More than you could ever hope to know."

I laughed. "I doubt that."

"What do you know about bicycles?" she asked. "Seriously. What could you possibly even need a bike for?

Let me guess. Judging by your ratty hair and baggy clothes, you want to rent a mountain bike."

I didn't reply.

"I knew it!" Hú Dié said. "I bet you don't have a clue where to ride. There are no mountains in this neighborhood."

"I have information."

"What kind of information? You barely speak Chinese."

"I have a GPS unit."

"Ha! That won't even get you to the foothills, let alone actual mountains for a mountain bike. You can never count on the roads being open around here. You would have to ask the locals how to get where you want to go, and you won't be able to speak their dialect. Many of them don't even speak Mandarin."

I said nothing.

"So, where is it you are going?" she asked.

"I have a better question," I replied. "Why am I wasting my time talking with you?"

She flashed that brilliant smile of hers. "Because you like me."

I felt my face turning red again.

"No need to be embarrassed," she said. "It happens to most guys. I'll tell you what: I will go with you and be your guide. I know which roads are open. It will be fun. I won't even charge you for borrowing a bike."

"You really are crazy," I said. "You don't even know me. *I* could be psycho."

"I doubt it. You're harmless."

I ground my teeth. "You can't come with me."

"Sure I can. I'll just close up the shop for a couple days. A ride in the mountains usually takes more than a single afternoon around here. If the shop gets an order for some bikes, my father can take care of it. It's my summer vacation, after all. I deserve a short getaway."

"If you want a getaway, go by yourself."

"It's more fun to ride with someone else."

"Why me?"

Hú Dié paused. "Honestly?"

"Yeah."

"I want to study in America someday, remember? You're American."

I nodded. "I see. You think by riding with me, we'll become friends and I'll help you go to college in the United States?"

"I don't know. Maybe. Even if you can't help me or you decide that you don't want to help me, so what? At least I'll have a fun ride in the mountains and get to practice my English."

I shook my head. "You don't understand. This is something that I have to do alone."

"Stop being so dramatic," Hú Dié said. "You can't do this alone. How are you supposed to accomplish anything if you barely even speak the language? I can be your interpreter. What have you got to lose?"

"The answer is still no."

"What's wrong?" she asked, growing feisty again. "Is it that you are afraid you won't be able to keep up with

a girl? Maybe you *should* be worried. I ride the mountains whenever I get the chance. I am good. Very good."

I took a deep breath and thought about what she was
saying. Maybe I would be better off with her coming
along. Beyond speaking the language and having knowledge of the roads and mountain terrain, she definitely
seemed to know bikes. Equipment broke all the time on
mountain trails. More than that, riding with a buddy was
simply responsible mountain biking. Anything could happen out there. Just because she went along did not mean
I had to tell her what I was up to.

"Well?" Hú Dié pressed. "It's getting late, and this is
not a safe city after dark. I'll tell you what—if you let me
go with you tomorrow, you can sleep here in the shop
tonight. I live upstairs with my father, and it will be easy
enough for you and me to leave first thing in the morning
from here. I will even throw in dinner tonight. You won't
find a better deal than that in this city. What do you say?"

I closed my eyes and thought about the encounter I'd
just had on the street. She was right. This city wasn't safe,
and I wouldn't find a better deal anywhere.

I decided to take a chance. After all, she was only a
girl. I opened my eyes and nodded.

And just like that, I had a new riding partner.

The question was, how safe was *she*?

I spent the rest of the evening in the bike shop, toggling through screens on the GPS unit while Hú Dié cooked dinner upstairs. When she finally came down, I was so hungry I could have eaten scrap metal.

Fortunately, I didn't have to. She had made a huge bowl of pork wontons in chicken broth with fresh napa cabbage and sliced pickled ginger on the side. It was delicious. We ate with metal chopsticks while sitting side by side at a grease-streaked workbench strewn with bike parts. Pretty much an ideal dinner setting. When she wasn't being feisty, Hú Dié was actually fun to be around. I even stopped getting that strange, nervous feeling when she was close to me.

We talked some, and I learned that while she lived here with her father, her mother lived elsewhere. I didn't ask why. Like me, she had no other family.

Hú Dié's father was out for the evening on business, and he didn't make it home as she'd expected. We ended up eating the bowl of food she'd set aside for him, too. By the time we'd finished, my hunger was more than satisfied. I pushed our empty bowls aside and handed Hú Dié the GPS unit, showing her the route that PawPaw had laid out for me. Both kilometers and miles were displayed.

"No problem," she said after looking things over. "This route appears to be programmed primarily for travel by bus, but we will be riding bikes, so we can take some shortcuts."

"Really?" I asked.

Hú Dié nodded. "I know roads through several small villages where buses don't go. This route shows sixty miles to the trailhead, but I can cut it down to about forty-five. We should be able to make it to the trailhead in four or five hours at a moderate pace."

"What about the trail itself?"

"It appears to be ten miles one way into the mountains. I have ridden out there several times, and we're probably going to have to spend the night. Those ten miles will take a couple hours, both going out and coming back. From what I remember, though, there is nothing at the final destination but a small, empty valley. Why would you want to go to that place?"

I'd been expecting this question. I had decided that since she would be with me the whole ride, I might as well tell her about the ruins. Of course, I wouldn't tell her *why* I wanted to go there. As for the man I was supposed to find, I would deal with that topic when the time came.

"There was a temple in that location," I said. "It was destroyed a long time ago."

"Cangzhen Temple?" she asked.

My eyes widened. "Yes! How do you know about Cangzhen?"

"I don't know much, only the few things my father has told me. There is supposed to be a crazy old hermit who lives in the temple ruins, but no one knows exactly where the ruins are located. Are you sure that's the spot?"

I couldn't believe my good luck. Her already knowing about the man would make things much easier. "I'm fairly sure that is the location. The person who programmed the GPS said it might not be exact, but it should be close."

She shrugged. "I guess the ruins could be in that valley. I've ridden all over those mountains except down there, and I've never come across any destroyed temples anywhere else."

"Do you know anything more about the hermit?"

"Not really. My father spends a fair amount of time in one of the villages out that way, and he hears things. People see the old man a few times a year, buying food and other supplies. My father said that he saw him once, and that he didn't look crazy at all, just really big. Maybe people only call him crazy because he prefers to be alone, or because he often talks to himself about the glory days of Cangzhen Temple. I've never heard stories about him being dangerous or anything."

"That's good."

"Do you want to talk with him or something?"

"Maybe. I just want to find the ruins first. Do you know anything more about Cangzhen?"

"There are legends, but they seem pretty unbelievable. Can I ask why you want to find it?"

"No. I don't mean to be rude, but it's personal."

"Fine," she snapped, her feistiness rising once more. "Be that way." She grabbed the dirty dishes.

I stood. "Here, let me help with those."

"No. I'd rather you didn't come upstairs. I'll take care of it." She headed up a staircase at the back of the shop. She returned a few minutes later with a couple of old blankets and a threadbare pillow. She handed them to me.

"I apologize for the condition of these," she said, stern-faced.

"These are great," I replied, trying to lighten the mood. "They are much better than what I had on the bus, which was nothing. Thank you."

"You're welcome. Do you think you will have a problem spending the night in the mountains tomorrow?"

"Not at all. I love camping. My grandfather takes me sometimes."

"Good. I enjoy it, too." She looked over at my backpack. "Do you have anything smaller?"

"I have a small duffel bag, but I don't think it's going to help much on a ride."

"I have a pack that you can use. What about riding pants?"

I frowned. "No. I had planned to hike to the ruins. I

didn't think of riding a bike there until I came into your shop."

Hú Dié sighed. "You at least brought short pants, right?"

"Yes. Several pairs. Why?"

"Give me one."

"What?"

"Just do it."

I rummaged through my backpack and pulled out a pair of brown cargo shorts. I tossed them to her.

"These will work," she said. "Now get some sleep. You are probably jet-lagged, and we have a long day ahead of us tomorrow."

"If you say so."

"I *do* say so," she said, "and from this point forward, you will do exactly as I say. If you think Kaifeng is a dangerous place, you should see some of the villages and mountain trails."

I groaned. "So I've been told."

"This is serious. Do you agree to listen to me or not?"

"Agreed."

Hú Dié nodded and turned away. "Good night then, Phoenix."

"Good night, Iron Butterfly."

She left, and I spread out my makeshift bed. As I lay down among the bicycles, I wondered what the heck I had just gotten myself into.

I slept very little that night. I wanted to blame my wakefulness on the time difference and the eight hours I'd slept on the bus, but I knew there was more. Not only did I have concerns about Hú Dié, who had just pushed her way into my life, I was also worried about Grandfather. He had appeared more or less okay when I left, but he was extremely tough, and he had always had a face of stone. It was impossible to tell how he really felt. He could be in agony and no one would know it. I looked forward to calling him as soon as the ride to Cangzhen Temple was over. I was dying to know how he was doing. It took me a long time to fall asleep.

I woke to something having dropped onto my face. I scrambled to sit up, finding that the object was the cargo shorts I'd given Hú Dié the night before.

"Try them on," Hú Dié said, hovering over me. "I hope they fit. I do not want to have to make another pair. I spent half the night working on them."

I examined the shorts and found that she had sewn padding into them. I didn't know what to say. Like many riders, I felt that padded riding shorts were a rider's most important piece of equipment outside of a helmet.

"Thank you," I said. "They look awesome, just like you'd find in a store."

"They are better than you would find in a store. Now put them on. I'll turn around."

Hú Dié turned away, and I hurriedly changed into the shorts, embarrassed. I squatted a few times. "You're right. These are better than anything I've tried from a store. They are really comfortable, like they were custom-made for me."

"They *were* custom-made for you."

"Oh, yeah. Thanks a lot."

"Can I turn around now?"

"Sure, sorry."

Hú Dié turned and looked me up and down. "The shorts do fit you well," she said. "Now let's see how I do with a bike. Do you still like that blue and white full-suspension? The one with the welds you questioned?"

I nodded.

"How do you like your ride? Firm? Soft?"

"I like my front forks firm," I said. "I've never ridden a bike with a rear suspension, so I don't know what to tell you about the rear shock absorber adjustment. I ride a hard-tail back home."

"Don't you like shocks?"

"I can't afford full suspension. I've always wanted to try one, though."

"Well, now is your chance. Hard-tails are good for smooth tracks with small hills and lots of turns. More of your energy is transferred to the rear wheel instead of being absorbed by the rear suspension. However, on rocky trails in the mountains like we're going to ride, full suspension is the way to go, especially over long distances. Your butt will thank you."

"My butt already thanks *you* for the padding," I joked.

Hú Dié rolled her eyes, but she cracked a smile. She went behind the tall counter and returned with a handful of hex wrenches, motioning for me to follow her over to the blue and white mountain bike. She began making adjustments, looking back and forth several times between the bike and me as she worked. I'd never seen someone work so quickly. First, she raised the seat post and adjusted the seat angle. Then she changed the angle of the handlebars and repositioned the brake levers. She even moved the gearshift thumb toggles to a slightly different location.

"Don't you need to measure me before you make those changes?" I asked.

"No. I am very good at judging dimensions just by looking at things." She grabbed a small, specialized hand pump to adjust the air pressure within the bike's rear shock absorber, which isolated the rear tire from the frame. "How much do you weigh?" she asked. "A hundred thirty pounds?"

"One-fifteen."

Hú Dié grinned. "So, the phoenix is as light as a bird? Maybe you will be able to fly with me, after all."

"Count on it, Butterfly."

She laughed and adjusted the shock's air pressure; then she inspected the tires.

"Are those tires tubeless?" I asked.

"Of course, and I've already treated the inner walls with sealant. We will bring inner tubes as backup in case we get a pinch flat on the trail or pick up a nail on the road that the sealant can't handle. I've also got several patch kits and a small hand pump. Nothing worse than being miles from anywhere with a flat tire."

"Agreed," I said. I watched as she checked the pressure in the tires by squeezing them between her thumb and forefinger.

"Don't you need a tire-pressure gauge for that?"

"No. Feels like forty-five pounds of air pressure in each, give or take a pound. That's good for riding city streets. Once we hit the trail, I'll drop it down to about thirty-five for better traction. Care to stick a gauge on them now and make a wager to see whether or not I'm right?"

"Nope."

She smiled. "Didn't think so. You're a fast learner. I'm assuming that if you didn't bring riding pants, you don't have riding shoes, either?"

I pointed to my hiking boots across the room. "Just those."

"I'll take care of it. Go put them on."

She headed behind the counter again while I went and put on my boots. I walked back to the bike, pulling its rear tire out of the stand that had been holding it upright. Mountain bikers *never* use kickstands. I checked the bike over closer than I had yesterday and liked what I saw, particularly the front and rear disc brakes. Low-end bikes have old-fashioned brake pads that compress against the wheel rims to slow the bike down. High-end bikes like the one I was looking at have a metal disc attached to each wheel down by the hub. Small metal calipers squeeze the disc with tremendous hydraulic-assisted force, like you'd find on a motorcycle. The stopping power of disc brakes is amazing and is sometimes necessary to prevent a rider from doing something tragic like coasting over a rocky bluff instead of pulling up short of it.

I climbed onto the bike and couldn't believe how well

it fit me. Hú Dié was very good. I bounced up and down a few times with my butt planted on the seat to test the rear suspension. It seemed as if it had about five inches' travel, which felt completely alien. Every time I pressed down and felt the bike give way beneath me, I swore the frame was snapping in half. I didn't like the sensation at all.

I stood, keeping my hands on the handle grips, and leaned out over the handlebars, pressing down. The shock-absorbing front fork gave way much like my bike at home, which made me feel better.

Hú Dié returned with a large pedal wrench and a pair of flats—traditional pedals like you would find on a regular kid's bike. You didn't need special shoes for these, and they were perfect for situations where you needed to put your foot down in a hurry. However, they were very inefficient, which was why Hú Dié was also carrying a pair of "cages" that could be attached to the tops of the pedals. I would be able to slip my feet into the cages to take advantage of the full range of pedaling motion, pulling up and around on the pedals just as much as pushing down. The drawback was that cages could be dangerous. Shoes sometimes got stuck in them while you were trying to pull your foot out to prevent yourself from tipping over.

Hú Dié looked down at the cages. "You want them?"

"Sure."

"You're a brave man."

"Sometimes."

I climbed off the bike and held it for Hú Dié as she

threaded the pedals onto the bike's drive sprocket crank arms and tightened them down. Then she attached the cages.

"I'll let you adjust the cage straps yourself," she said. "I don't want to be responsible for you snapping your ankle because you couldn't get your foot out in time."

"No problem," I said. "Thanks."

"Don't thank me yet. Adjust your cages. I have to grab a few more things."

I straddled the bike again and began to make the adjustments while Hú Dié headed back upstairs. When she came down, I hardly recognized her. Her long hair was pulled back into a ponytail. A battered riding helmet and a pair of killer sunglasses hid most of her face, while a short-sleeved pink riding jersey showed off her normally hidden buff arms. She also wore a short, floppy green plaid skirt over tight black riding shorts that went all the way down to her knees. It was a combo that I'd seen girls wearing in cycling magazines; however, neither the skirt nor the riding shorts could hide the fact that she was a total *quaddess*. Those thighs would give any guy back home a run for his money.

I looked down at her shoes and smiled. Her pink mountain bike cleats were scuffed and torn. Hú Dié was hard-core.

She held out a fresh-from-the-box helmet and an old hydration backpack. "The backpack should hold enough water, snacks, and clothes for an overnight trip for both of us," she said. "I've already filled the water bladder. As for the brain bucket, I believe it should fit your fat head."

"Very funny. Thanks for loaning me the gear." I noticed that she wasn't wearing a hydration pack. "What are you going to drink?"

"I have water bottle cages on my bike, plus a couple more bottles and some energy bars in my jersey pockets. My extra clothes are in the pack, though, along with two space blankets and other supplies. Wearing the pack is what you get for not bringing your own gear."

"I don't mind," I said, climbing off the bike. I placed its rear wheel back into the bike stand and took the pack and helmet from Hú Dié. The pack was surprisingly heavy. She turned for a moment, and I saw that the huge pockets sewn into the lower back region of her riding jersey bulged with two full water bottles and whatever else she had in them. I put on the helmet and found that it fit perfectly. Even the chinstrap had been adjusted to the ideal length.

"Thank you," I said.

"Thank me again, and I'll knock you out," Hú Dié said. "The more you say it, the less it means."

My brow furrowed. She sounded just like Grandfather. "Whatever you say, boss."

"Follow me," she ordered, "and bring the bike." She went to the front door, opening it for me.

"Just a minute," I said, and hurried over to my own backpack. I grabbed the GPS unit, dropping it into one of the cargo pockets on my riding shorts. Then I snatched a change of clothes to sleep in and shoved them into Hú Dié's pack along with my passport and wallet. I slipped the pack onto my shoulders, adjusted the straps, slung the hydration hose and mouthpiece forward over my shoulder, and grabbed the bike.

"Heads up!" Hú Dié said.

I got a hand up in time to catch an energy bar just before it hit my face. *What was it with Chinese women throwing food at me?*

"Good reflexes," she said. "Eat that now. I already had one."

I ripped the wrapper open with my teeth and headed for the door.

Outside, Hú Dié locked the front door behind us. The early morning air was crisp. I followed her to a small loading dock, and she unlocked a large metal door, rolling it up like a gigantic shade. The loading bay behind the door was empty except for a mud-streaked neon-pink mountain bike unlike any I had ever seen. It was leaning against a wall, its frame all odd angles and strange bends. Its component configuration looked like something from a parallel universe. Where you would normally find the front and rear shocks of a full-suspension bike, I saw rigid welds. Where you would expect to find rigid welds, I saw shocks. The only things I recognized as typical were two water bottle cages, but even they were bolted on in odd locations. I supposed there was a rationale behind all of this, but I couldn't see it. The engineering was beyond me.

"That's Trixie," Hú Dié said, her face beaming with pride. "She's my baby. I rode her yesterday and haven't had a chance to give her a bath."

I was horrified. "You *named* your bike?"

"Of course."

"That's too weird."

"No, it's not. Do you like her?"

I scratched my chin. "I don't know. I think she may be a little too tricked-out for my taste."

"See, I told you I knew more about bike design than you ever would." She walked over to her bike. "Trixie is revolutionary."

"She looks complicated."

"She is." Hú Dié climbed onto her bike and clipped into the pedals. "Trixie is complicated and beautiful and temperamental. Just like me." She flashed a radiant smile and shot off like a pink cannonball, calling out, "Catch me if you can, Phoenix!"

I half expected her to turn around, to show she was joking with me, but she didn't.

I needed no further prompting. I jammed my feet into the pedal cages and took off after the complicated girl on the tricked-out pink bicycle.

12

I wove in and out of city traffic for at least five miles before I finally caught up with Hú Dié. She was never more than a few hundred yards ahead, but she was fast enough on the streets that I wasn't able to get to her sooner. I had to admit, she had some serious skills. I couldn't wait to get into more open country to put the hurt on her. I hated riding in the city, especially here.

There were few traffic lights and even fewer stop signs. Aggressive drivers zoomed in and out of lanes at will. Several times, I had to blast up a curb to avoid being run down. I would rather have taken the sidewalk, but that was impossible because many storekeepers used the entire width of the walk in front of their shops to sell their goods.

Once I had caught Hú Dié, she slowed her pace. She was breathing hard, and trickles of sweat shimmered down the backs of her calves and the nape of her neck. She was pushing herself, but unlike me, she was enjoying it.

The traffic began to thin, and I started having a better time. We rode for miles in silence, side by side. The storefronts grew farther and farther apart, until the city gave way to small, dusty fields. From there, the landscape changed to larger, more open spaces like I'd seen from the bus. The air freshened and became noticeably cleaner, and the sun rose higher. It was pleasant, but it was going to get hot soon.

I watched Hú Dié slowly drain her water bottles while I sipped from the hydration pack's long tube. After an hour, I pulled the GPS unit from my cargo riding shorts' pocket and saw that we had traveled more than fourteen miles—pretty good time for a mountain bike.

I also saw that Hú Dié had set us on a shorter path, just like she'd said she would. The GPS's auto-routing software had adjusted to our current location and was showing that we were still headed in the right direction, yet we had shaved a good distance off the original route. I noticed a large dot on the map and realized that we were coming up to a village. I asked Hú Dié about it.

"It is very small," she said. "Hardly worth mentioning. We will be through it in five minutes."

She was right. The village was little more than a cluster of old two-story buildings made from yellow mud bricks. Every hundred yards or so along one whole side of the road, I saw huge white circles on the ground, each more than twenty feet in diameter. We swerved around several before I realized what they were—low piles of rice being dried in the sun.

The asphalt on which the rice was lying was likely very good for drying because it was black and absorbed heat, but it was also coated with dirt and stained with oil and gas and who knew what else from the rusted, leaking vehicles that passed over this road. I now understood why Grandfather made me triple-wash every batch of rice we cooked. Even though this rice was probably only going to be eaten by locals and would never make it to Indiana, I wasn't sure I could ever bring myself to touch another bowlful again.

Not only did the rice make me uneasy, the people here did, too. They were none too friendly. Nearly every person we passed seemed to be simply standing around, and all of them stared at us. None offered so much as a wave, even after I waved first. I was glad when we were out of there.

We rode on for three more hours in comfortable silence, passing through two more villages nearly identical to the first, all the way down to the circles of rice in the road. Our tires hummed monotonously over hot, pot-holed pavement, and I began to itch for some challenging terrain.

Finally, the topography began to change, and I grew excited. We had reached the foothills. I wiped sweat from my eyes and checked the GPS unit again. So far, so good. We'd traveled forty miles, and if Hú Dié's estimate was correct, we were just a few miles from the trailhead. I was beginning to feel a little fatigued, but the shift in scenery and terrain was helping to energize me.

With the foothills came another village, and as we approached, I saw with relief that this one was noticeably different from the others. It contained buildings constructed of stone instead of mud bricks, and the inhabitants seemed much friendlier. They bustled about with activity, smiling and waving vigorously as we rode past. I saw several old men leading oxen, and a few young men driving trucks loaded with baskets of tea leaves.

The mountains beyond the foothills looked much bigger in person than in the pictures I'd seen on the Internet. While the hills I rode back in Indiana rose more than one thousand feet, these were much higher. The range was called Song Shan, and it was famous for being the location of the legendary Shaolin Temple. Hú Dié must have noticed my apprehension, because she giggled and punched me in the arm, nearly knocking me off my bike.

"Hey!" I said.

"Afraid to fly high?" she asked. "Perhaps you are more like a chicken than a phoenix?"

I frowned and tried to think of a sarcastic comeback in her native language, but nothing came to mind. Someday, I would have to learn to trash-talk in Chinese.

As we reached the far end of the village, Hú Dié turned into a small park and stopped beside an ancient-looking well. I stopped beside her, and we both climbed off our bikes. She began pulling an old bucket up by a tattered rope while I grabbed her empty water bottles and popped off the siphon tops. I held the plastic bottles on the edge of the well's thigh-high brick rim, and she filled them. We made a good team, neither one saying a word, yet both knowing full well what the other was going to do next.

Until that moment, I'd never considered what it might be like to have a sister. I thought it might feel similar to what I was feeling now. Here was a girl who irritated me some of the time, but who could also be like a good friend. I was curious to see how the rest of this ride would go.

After capping the last bottle, I removed the pack and set it on the ground with a loud *CLANK!*

"My stuff must have shifted," Hú Dié said. She elbowed me out of the way and opened the pack.

"What have you got in there?" I asked.

"Tools, mostly. I also have some spare parts. There aren't any bike shops out here." She sighed. "I'm going to have to repack everything."

Hú Dié began pulling stuff out of the pack, and I took the GPS out of my pocket.

"Here," Hú Dié said, holding out the pack's empty water bladder. "Fill this first."

I set the GPS unit on a rock next to Hú Dié and did as she ordered. As I was working, I kept glancing at a little building about thirty yards away. She must have seen me staring at it.

"Restroom," she said.

"Awesome," I replied, handing her the full bladder. "Be right back." I headed for the building as she continued to reposition things inside the pack.

I was just finishing up my business inside the building

when I heard a man's voice outside. I didn't catch what he said, but he was talking to Hú Dié in Mandarin. She replied by saying that she was on a bike trip with her friend.

I stepped out of the building and saw an older man standing in front of her. She was squatting next to the backpack with both hands inside it. I caught movement out of the corner of my eye and saw a second man hurrying toward Hú Dié from behind, his eyes glued to the GPS unit on the rock beside her.

"Hú Dié, watch your back!" I shouted.

Hú Dié turned her head, and the man in front of her grabbed her ponytail. She wailed like a banshee, and for a second, we all froze. Then Hú Dié rocketed to her feet, driving the top of her helmeted head into the bottom of her attacker's chin. The man stumbled backward, releasing her ponytail, and she pulled her hands out of the pack.

Hú Dié had wrapped a section of spare bike chain around her right fist. I began to run toward her as she leaped forward, slamming her iron fist into the face of the still-stumbling man. His body went rigid as a board, and he crashed to the ground.

The second man was now running toward Hú Dié, but his eyes were still on the GPS unit. I was certain that I'd get to him before he got to it. I was within a few strides of the man when Hú Dié shouted, "Phoenix, jump!"

I glanced at her and saw that she'd unwound the bike chain from her fist. She was swinging it over her head like a whip.

"JUMP!"

I jumped less than an arm's length away from the second attacker. Hú Dié swung the chain down, and the end struck the man's leg, wrapping around his ankle. He howled and tripped, and I kicked him in the chest as I came back to earth. Hú Dié let go of the chain and the kick sent him reeling toward the well, his thighs colliding with the brick rim. He toppled into the hole headfirst. There was a *SPLASH!* and the sound of thrashing. The man shouted in Mandarin, "I can't swim!"

I grabbed the GPS unit and ran to the well. I looked down and saw the man flailing about, pressing his hands against the brick-lined sides in an effort to keep his head above water. I shoved the GPS into one of my cargo pockets and grabbed the bucket, lowering it with an ancient winch.

"What are you doing?" Hú Dié said as she hurried to the backpack. "We need to get out of here! These guys probably have friends."

"We can't just leave him down there," I said. "He'll drown."

"Forget him. We need to take care of ourselves." Hú Dié began to stuff everything into the backpack.

The bucket reached the man, and he frantically grabbed it. I checked to make sure the rope was secure and that the winch would hold. It seemed strong enough. When I looked back down, he was beginning to climb the rope.

Hú Dié was already on her bike, pedaling away.

"Hey!" I shouted. I grabbed the pack and jumped on my bike as the guy climbed out of the well. He shook his fist at me.

I hit the road.

I caught up with Hú Dié and saw that her helmet had a deep dent from the first guy's chin. She also had marks on her hand from the bike chain.

"Why did you leave?" I asked.

Hú Dié scowled. "I *told* you to listen to me during this ride, you idiot."

"But that guy could have died!"

"You don't know that."

"He couldn't swim!"

"It's a small village. Someone would have heard his shouts."

"I don't agree."

"I don't care."

"But—"

"Shut up and ride!"

She began to accelerate.

I shook my head. That had to be the most famous saying in mountain biking.

It took some effort, but I caught Hú Dié again, and then I passed her. The surprised look on her face made me feel good. I held the lead until the road became a narrow line of dirt that wound its way through the foot-hills, toward the mountains. I continued up the trail and turned to look at Hú Dié, but she wasn't there.

I hit the brakes and spun around. I pedaled hard back

the way I'd come, catching sight of Hú Dié waiting for me on a side trail. That must have been her way of making a point. She was the leader out here.

Point taken.

We let some air out of our tires for better off-road traction as Hú Dié said we would, and we continued. She set a grueling pace for about two miles, then eased off. I soon saw why. The trail swept sharply up toward the first peak, and the compacted earth we had been riding on was now covered with a thick layer of small stones that had washed down from higher elevations.

I shifted to an easier gear and allowed a large gap to open between us. Our back tires had begun to slip on the loose stones, and Hú Dié's powerful legs were blasting marble-sized rocks up behind her. The last thing I needed was one of those in my eye. I wished I had my riding goggles.

Halfway up the peak, the loose rock layer thinned before finally disappearing altogether. From here on up, I guessed it would be nothing but large boulders and solid sheets of stone. I was right. Surprisingly, though, a clearly defined trail was still evident. After half an hour of steady climbing, we reached the top of the peak and took a short break to catch our breath and drink some water. Hú Dié didn't say a word.

The view was spectacular. All around us were mountain slopes. This region was famous for a certain kind of tea, and I expected to find the area covered with tea plantations. Instead, I saw only small clumps of pine trees, low grass, and lots of rock. The tea must grow elsewhere.

I checked the GPS and saw that we were still on course. Approximately seven miles to go. I switched the unit over to its altitude function and found that we were currently two thousand feet above sea level—higher than I'd ever ridden before, but not so high that the altitude affected my lungs or made me light-headed.

Hú Dié pointed southwest and broke her silence. "See those five peaks? The valley we want is between the fourth and fifth."

My eyes followed Hú Dié's finger. Our destination looked a long way off, but at least I didn't see any peaks higher than the one we were currently on, or any valleys that were really deep. "How is the rest of the ride?" I asked.

"Pretty much just like this. We should be there in a couple of hours. Do you think you can make it?"

"Of course."

"You're a much better rider than I was expecting."

"Thanks, I think. You're very good, too." I checked my watch. It was nearly noon. We were going to have to spend the night at the ruins for sure. At least we were now on speaking terms.

Hú Dié lowered her seat in preparation for the long descent, and I did the same. We took off down the hill, and I welcomed the rush of air that blasted through my helmet vents. The grade was steep enough that I didn't have to pedal, but I still had to pay attention, steering my bike over and around obstacles. The shocks on this full-suspension bike made the job of cruising down the mountain easier, and I knew my body was taking much less abuse over the jarring terrain than it would have with my hard-tail bike back home. Even so, I didn't like the way the bike sagged on big drops. It felt as if the frame were held together with rubber bands. I would take my bike in Indiana over this one any day.

We reached the bottom and stopped just long enough to raise our seats before beginning the climb up the second peak. Once we reached the second summit, we repeated our water break and seat lowering before continuing down to follow the same sequence up, over, and down the third and fourth peaks. The trail forked a few times, but Hú Dié always seemed to know which way to go without consulting the GPS.

When we finally arrived in the valley between the fourth and fifth peaks, Hú Dié pulled over. She was breathing hard, and so was I. She asked me to take out the GPS unit, and we both had long drinks and ate more energy bars while we got our bearings. I checked my watch again. It was 2:30 p.m.

I glanced around, comparing what I saw to the GPS unit's topographical map. The trail we were on continued up the slope of the fifth peak, which was evident both in real life and on the digital display. However, the GPS showed that we should veer off the trail into unmarked forest to get to the destination that PawPaw had programmed. The trees were fairly thick in that direction and the ground was covered with large ferns, but it wasn't so dense that an experienced mountain biker couldn't blaze his or her own trail.

I turned to Hú Dié, who was looking over my shoulder at the GPS. "What do you think?" I asked.

"If the temple is somewhere in those trees, I now understand why I've never seen it. I've never had a reason to go in there. How far off this trail is it supposed to be?"

"The GPS shows less than a mile."

"No problem," she said. "I can ride through that stuff. How about you?"

"No problem."

"Perfect. I'll lead."

"Uh . . . no. I don't think so."

"Excuse me?"

"I appreciate you helping me get this far. I really do. But I prefer to go in there alone."

I thought I could feel Hú Dié glaring at me from behind her sunglasses. "That wasn't the deal we made," she said.

"All right, how about you give me a half-hour head start so I can spend a little time there alone."

"How about ten minutes."

"Twenty minutes."

"No. Ten minutes or nothing."

I set my jaw. "Fine. Ten minutes." I shoved the GPS unit back into my pocket, took one more swig of water, and tore into the trees.

I plowed through the shadowy undergrowth, the spokes of my wheels shredding waist-high ferns into sticky green confetti. Bits of fern frond stuck to my bare legs and bike frame, while small sticks thrown up by my front tire wedged themselves into my drive sprocket and pedal cages. It was going to take hours to clean all of this gunk out of the bike's mechanical components.

I rolled and rocked at a breakneck pace around massive elm trees like a soldier running through a minefield. I continued my frantic pedaling, hoping that when Hú Dié began to ride, she would follow at a more reasonable pace. Perhaps I could stretch my ten minutes of alone time into fifteen or twenty. I blasted ahead for another several minutes before I noticed a change in the forest.

The gigantic elms that I'd been riding through gave way to noticeably younger trees that were fewer and farther between. I guessed that this was the work of people, namely someone who lived in temple ruins and burned firewood to stay warm in winter. I had to be getting close.

I slowed to a stop and slipped my left foot out of its pedal cage, resting my foot on the ground. I pulled out the GPS unit and found that I was pretty much exactly on top of the spot PawPaw had identified as being near the temple. I put the GPS away and removed my helmet. I also slipped off the hydration pack, draping both items over my handlebars. With a stealthy approach on foot, I might be able to learn a few things about the man I had been sent to locate, before we met face to face. I looked over my shoulder, listening for signs of Hú Dié and trying to decide whether I should hide the bike, when I realized something was wrong. The forest was absolutely silent.

Normally, a mountain biker ripping through an area doesn't leave silence in his or her wake. Birds shriek and squirrels chatter angrily, each scolding the intruder in their own language. The animals do this from a safe distance, so even if my stopping had silenced the critters nearest to me, in less than a minute they would have put plenty of space between me and them, and then they would have let me have it. Their silence meant someone else was on the move, and it wasn't Hú Dié. I didn't hear her.

I looked back toward the new-growth area and found myself staring at the tip of a wicked-looking spear blade looming an inch from my forehead. I reacted without thinking. I dropped the bike and shifted all of my weight to my left foot—the one on the ground—and instinctively rotated the heel of my other foot to release it from the pedal clip. Unfortunately, I wasn't using clip-in pedals on this ride. I was using pedal cages.

I fell down. I remembered the pedal cage and jerked my foot free, silently cursing myself. I rolled onto my back, trying to put some distance between myself and whoever was holding that spear, but it was no use. The spear tip flashed downward, stopping half an inch above my thumping heart.

"Stand," a deep voice commanded in Mandarin.

As I stood, the spear tip followed me the whole way up.

"Who are you?" the voice asked in Mandarin.

I understood this, too, but I didn't answer. Instead, I focused beyond the spear tip for the first time. I saw an impossibly old man with the physique of an NFL linebacker.

The man was well over six feet tall, with shoulders as wide as a doorway. He wore a tattered orange robe, beneath which I could see a thick chest. The skin on his bald head sagged with age, and his face was covered with liver spots the size of silver dollars. His eyes were as bright as PawPaw's, and he stared at me. Unlike PawPaw, though, who appeared to search for kindness, this man sought weakness. I knew better than to look away. I locked eyes with him, my irises flashing green fire.

The old man nodded as if I had passed some kind of test, and he lowered his spear. The breeze picked up, and I caught a familiar scent in the air. The man was sweating, and he smelled just like Grandfather and PawPaw. This had to be the guy I was supposed to find.

The old monk spoke again in Mandarin. "Answer my question, young man. Who are you?"

I bowed and replied in English. "My name is Phoenix Collins. I've come in search of Cangzhen Temple. Do you speak English? I am sorry, but my Chinese is very poor."

The man glowered and answered in English. "I speak your language. You are American?"

"Yes, sir."

"What does an American know about Cangzhen?"

"Not very much. My grandfather sent me to find it, and a monk who may live within its ruins. Are you the man I am looking for?"

"Who is your grandfather?"

"His name is Chénjí Long—Silent Dragon. We live in the state of Indiana, but he spent his life in China until thirteen years ago, when he moved to the United States to take care of me. He said he lived at Cangzhen Temple when he was a boy."

The old man slowly shook his head, as though he were unhappy. He seemed to drift into deep thought, and I turned my attention to the spear's metal tip. It was almost a foot long and cut into a wavy pattern. It was nasty. I had seen one like it many times. It was a snake-head spear, and it was Grandfather's favorite weapon.

The old man's mind appeared to return to the moment, and he said, "I know who you are, and I can probably guess why you have come. I never expected to meet you, Phoenix. Something must be very wrong for you to be here. The Cangzhen Temple ruins are near. If you can prove yourself, I will show them to you."

I flinched. "What do you want me to do?"

The old man nodded at his spear.

A chill ran down my spine. I knew exactly what he wanted. He wanted me to show him that I knew how to fight by doing a kata, or form, with him—a series of practice moves. We weren't going to fight for real, but I needed to choose wisely nonetheless.

I dropped into a deep Horse Stance and thought quickly. I needed a kung fu form in which one person with a spear attacks another person who is empty-handed.

Say Sow Seh came to mind—"Four-Hand Snake." This form was representative of snake-style kung fu, which happened to be my favorite and the one I did best. Timing and precision would be critical, because one false move by either individual with even a practice spear could mean serious injury, and I had the scars to prove it. Doing the form with an unknown partner who was holding a sharpened spear—a snake-head spear, no less—was practically suicidal. I hoped he knew this form as well as I did. There was only one way to find out.

"*Say Sow Seh!*" I challenged.

The old monk smiled and attacked, his foot-long spear tip heading straight for my liver. I weaved out of the way like an undulating serpent. As he pulled the spear back, he sliced at my thigh, attempting to sever my femoral artery, but I spun clear, keeping low to the ground.

The spear tip changed direction suddenly, and the

old man thrust it at my back. I rolled forward, snaking around a tree as the razor-sharp blade barely missed me, cutting a wide swath of bark from an elm.

The old monk clearly knew the form, but he was playing for keeps. It made my blood boil. I emerged from behind the tree and spat like a cobra, raising my hands into snake-head fists.

The monk lifted the spear high over his head and began to spin it like a helicopter blade. Now it was my turn. I coiled and struck, lashing out at his abdomen with rigid fingers. I managed to hit my target before he could twist out of the way; however, I wished I hadn't. His stomach was as hard as steel.

"Ow!" I said.

As I shook my tingling hands, he took a swing at my head with the spinning spear. I nearly forgot to duck.

I rolled backward and popped to my feet. The monk stopped swinging the spear. I readied myself for the next attack, which would be at my throat, when I heard a bloodcurdling scream from behind the old man.

My eyes widened as Hú Dié burst through the trees atop Trixie, pulling a high-speed wheelie. The old monk turned to see what was going on, and Hú Dié rammed him square in the chest with Trixie's front tire. The monk went down awkwardly, the spear still in his hands.

Hú Dié released her grip on Trixie's handlebars and unclipped her shoes, jumping off her bike. She landed on top of the huge old man, who was lying on his back.

"Hú Dié, NO!" I shouted.

She didn't seem to hear. She clasped her hands

together over her head and dropped to her knees, swinging her arms down toward the monk's head as though she were swinging a sledgehammer.

The old man raised the thick spear shaft in front of his face to protect himself, but Hú Dié's forearms smashed through the shaft as if it were a number-two pencil. The monk moved his head just in time to dodge the rest of Hú Dié's brutal blow, which blasted an impressive crater in the dirt.

The old monk hissed like a dragon and shrugged Hú Dié off him. He sprang to his feet, and Hú Dié sprang to hers.

"Hú Dié!" I shouted again. "Stop! Everything is okay!"

Hú Dié shook her head as though clearing it of cobwebs. She turned to me. "Huh?"

I raised my arms in the universal gesture of surrender. "Everything is cool. He wasn't attacking me for real. We were just doing a two-man kung fu form."

Her eyes narrowed. "You know kung fu?"

"Yeah. I'm actually pretty good at it. Ask him." I pointed toward the old monk.

The old man nodded. "Phoenix is quite good, and so are you, young lady. That trick with the bicycle was ingenious, and you shattered my favorite spear with your bare arms. Iron Forearm training, I presume?"

Hú Dié stared hard at the old monk. "None of your business. Who are you?"

The monk seemed taken aback by her disrespectful response. For a moment, I thought he was going to club her with one of the broken spear halves. But then his face softened, and he lowered his voice.

"Fair enough," the old monk said. "Perhaps you do deserve some answers. You certainly have fought hard enough to earn them. Come, let me show you who I am."

Hú Dié and I followed the old monk through the patch of new-growth forest. The old man carried the broken halves of his spear, while Hú Dié and I pushed our bikes. My helmet and pack hung from my handlebars, banging against Hú Dié's dented helmet, which dangled from Trixie's handlebars. Her helmet was even more beat up than before. I turned to her.

"Thank you for coming to my . . . um . . . rescue," I said. "I appreciate it."

Hú Dié took off her sunglasses and glared at me. "The next time you go on a ride with someone, you stick with that person at all times, understand?"

"I know. It's just that . . ." My voice trailed off. I couldn't decide whether to tell her why I'd wanted to leave her behind, or why I'd even come here in the first place. I felt as if she deserved to know after she had just risked her life for me.

"It's just what?" she asked.

I hesitated. "I want to tell you something."

"So tell me."

I took a deep breath. "Have you ever heard of a substance called dragon bone?"

The old monk shot me a questioning look but said nothing.

Hú Dié looked from me to the monk, then back to me. She shook her head. "No. Is that why you came here?"

"Yes."

"What is it?"

"A kind of medicine."

"What does it do?"

"Basically, it helps people live longer—people like my grandfather. His remaining supply was stolen. If he doesn't get more soon, he will die."

The old monk stopped in his tracks. "Stolen?"

"Yes," I said. "Two guys came to our house. They took all of it."

"Who would do such a thing?" Hú Dié asked.

"I don't know. I was thinking Grandfather might have been mixed up with Triad gangsters or a secret society or something long ago. One of the guys was Chinese."

"Not the Triads," the old monk said. "Your grandfather would have nothing to do with them."

"Who could it be, then?"

"I do not know," the old man replied.

Hú Dié looked at the monk. "Do you have more of this dragon bone?"

"Before we discuss this any further," the old man said to Hú Dié, "I must insist that you tell me your name."

"Fine," she replied. "My name is Tiě Hú Dié. My father and I own a bicycle shop in Kaifeng."

The old man stared at her for a moment. He nodded and seemed to look at her with new eyes. "Iron Butterfly. That explains your powerful arms. Though I've never spoken with him, I know of your father. I also knew of your grandfather, and of your great-grandfather. Your family is well known in certain circles. You sell more than bicycles, do you not?"

"Sometimes."

The old man nodded. "To each his own. If your family knows how to do one thing, it is to keep secrets. I trust there is no harm in your hearing more of my conversation with Phoenix if you agree to never mention dragon bone to anyone."

"Of course," she said.

The old monk nodded again and turned to me. "You, either."

"Yes, sir," I said.

"Now that we have an understanding," the old monk said, "Long is *my* name, not your grandfather's."

"Excuse me?" I said.

"Your grandfather's real name is not Chénjí Long. It is Seh."

I was confused. *"Snake?"*

"Correct. Shame on him for disguising his serpentine lineage. Shame on him, too, for denying you yours. You clearly move like a member of that species, and you do it well."

"My grandfather is a good man," I said in a defensive tone. "I owe everything to him."

The old monk straightened. "I apologize if I have offended you. Your grandfather is indeed a very good man in many respects. On the other hand, he is also a stubborn, secretive individual who would rather run from his past than embrace it. Your family history is long and dark, Phoenix. While it may be your grandfather's nature to hide the truth from others, he should hide nothing from you. You are the last of his line. You are among the last of the Five Ancestors."

I felt my head begin to spin.

"Hold on a minute," Hú Dié said. "Are you saying that *Phoenix* is related to one of the Five Ancestors?"

The monk nodded. "He is, as am I. You both may call me Grandmaster Long. I am the last Dragon to come out of Cangzhen Temple."

Hú Dié's eyes widened. "So the legends are true? There really were five kids from this region who helped save China?"

"Yes."

"When?"

"It was the Year of the Tiger, 1650," Grandmaster Long said. "The children grew up right here."

I was having a difficult time taking all of this in. What were Hú Dié and Grandmaster Long talking about? I asked, "Who were the Five Ancestors?"

"*That* is a very long story," Grandmaster Long replied. "It will have to wait. First, we must address the dragon bone. How long has your grandfather been without it?"

I fought an overwhelming urge to push for more information and instead focused on Grandfather's current situation. "Almost five days," I said, "but he has an emergency supply of about a week's worth."

"You made it here quickly. I am impressed. I will do what I can for him. While he and I do not get along, I wish him no harm, and I value the fact that he sent you to me instead of infringing upon our mutual friend in Beijing. I am assuming PawPaw helped you find me."

"Yes. We wouldn't be here without her."

Grandmaster Long looked up at the midafternoon sun. "Then let us make sure you do not disappoint those who have brought you this far. You have no chance of making it back to Kaifeng before dark. I suggest you spend the night here and leave at first light, for your grandfather's sake. I will supply you with enough dragon bone to keep him in your life for as long as you and he wish. I like you, Phoenix. You have a good heart."

I had a hard time believing my ears. This really was going to work out. I blinked away a tear that was beginning to form and bowed. "Thank you, Grandmaster Long. Thank you so much."

"You are most welcome. Follow me to the temple and I shall show you what remains. Afterward, we will eat and I can tell you tales of Cangzhen Temple, if you would like."

"Please do!" Hú Dié said enthusiastically.

"Ditto that," I said.

Grandmaster Long smiled. "It pleases me to know that someone is interested in our history. I may as well begin the lesson right here, in this section of younger trees." He raised his arms wide, a broken spear half in each hand. "This ground was devoid of anything except ankle-high grass for hundreds of years. Monks like myself took great pains to keep it that way because it allowed us to see invaders and attack them before they attacked us. Not too long ago, I decided to stop maintaining it. I am afraid I'm getting too old for that kind of work."

He began to walk, leading us through the new-growth patch of forest for another seventy yards or so until we came to the remains of a stone wall that was at least seven feet tall. It was charred and crumbling, and entire sections were missing. Hú Dié and I leaned our bikes against the wall next to one of the larger gaps, which was wide enough for several people to walk through side by side.

I peered through the gap, taking in every detail. The wall had once surrounded a vast space filled with many one-story buildings of various sizes, all of which were made of stone and appeared to have been scorched by fire. Most of the buildings were crumbling, and nearly all had clay roof tiles that were cracked and broken. Cobblestone walks crisscrossed the ground, and some of the stones under the building eaves were splashed with black stains that I guessed had once been bloodred. This was no doubt the site of a horrific attack.

"Two hundred warrior monks died here," Grandmaster Long said in a solemn tone. "Muskets and cannons were new to China at the time. The monks did not stand a chance."

I looked at the damaged perimeter wall and couldn't help thinking about pictures I'd seen of the famous Shaolin Temple nearby. While Shaolin was called a temple, it was actually a walled compound containing multiple temples and other buildings in which several hundred people could live in isolation, just like Cangzhen. The Shaolin compound had also been destroyed, but it was recently rebuilt. Millions of people from all over the world now visit it each year.

"Why don't you rebuild Cangzhen like Shaolin has been?" I asked.

"I hope to," Grandmaster Long said. "China is changing, and the time may soon be right to push Cangzhen Temple out of the ashes. However, making it a tourist destination is not exactly what I had in mind."

"Yeah," Hú Dié said. "'Hidden Truth Temple' doesn't exactly sound like a vacation hot spot."

I remembered asking Grandfather about the temple's name and being told that I should ask here. I looked at Grandmaster Long. "What was hidden in this place?"

"Many things," he replied. "And nothing."

Hú Dié glanced suspiciously at Grandmaster Long. "What is it?" he asked.

"My father says the same thing whenever he does not want me to know something."

Grandmaster Long looked offended. "Do you not trust me?"

Hú Dié folded her arms. "You have done nothing to make me distrust you."

"But I have done nothing to earn your trust, either, have I?"

Hú Dié didn't respond.

"Fair enough," Grandmaster Long said. "It is wise for a young woman to be cautious of strangers. I will show you something to prove my good intentions. Wait here. I will be right back."

Grandmaster Long hurried deep into the compound, out of sight, and Hú Dié turned to me. "Do you trust this guy?"

"Why shouldn't I?"

"Because you just met him."

"I just met you, too."

She cocked her arm to punch me, but I stepped backward, out of her reach. She lowered her fist.

"What about your grandfather?" she asked. "Does he trust this guy?"

"I guess so. He sent me here alone, didn't he?"

She nodded. "I suppose you're right. Maybe I have mixed feelings about him because I just fought with him."

"Actually, it's my fault that you attacked him. I went off on my own, remember? Riders are supposed to stick together."

Hú Dié's eyes narrowed. "Don't remind me."

Grandmaster Long returned carrying an ornate

dragon-shaped vessel made of what looked like porcelain. I felt my pulse quicken. The container was a lot like the one Grandfather had used for his dragon bone, only much larger.

Grandmaster Long removed the vessel's lid and showed the contents to me and Hú Dié. There was several times more dragon bone than Grandfather had had.

"Dragon bone, I presume?" Hú Dié asked.

"Yes," Grandmaster Long replied. He looked at me. "I had planned to share this with you in the morning, but I will give you a portion for your grandfather now as an act of good faith and trust. I will find a suitable container and—" He stopped in midsentence, staring back the way we had come.

Hú Dié craned her neck, cocking her head to one side as if listening.

Then I heard it, too—the high-pitched whine of an off-road motorcycle, coming on fast. I looked down at the bits of fern frond still stuck to my legs. I had left a clear trail through the trees that anyone could follow. But who might be trailing us?

An instant later, I caught a glimpse of a motorcycle racing through the trees. It was traveling at an incredible speed. It reached the far edge of the new-growth section of elms, and I saw a second off-road motocross cycle coming up behind it. Both riders wore the reinforced racing jackets and tinted, full face mask helmets favored by sport bike motorcyclists. Even so, I could tell by their physiques exactly who they were.

It was Slim and Meathead.

15

I pointed into the trees and shouted, "It's the guys who stole my grandfather's dragon bone!"

"Take cover!" Grandmaster Long said.

We raced through the large gap in the wall. Hú Dié and I ducked behind the wall, while Grandmaster Long cradled the large dragon bone vessel under one arm like a rugby ball and headed for a small, windowless building about the size of a backyard storage shed. The shed had no door, but its four stone walls appeared solid, and most of its roof was intact.

One of the motorcycle engines revved, and I peeked through a crack in the wall to see Slim take off ahead of Meathead. The thin man zipped through the young trees like a motocross champion, powering through the gap in the wall as Grandmaster Long slipped into the shed.

Slim gunned his engine and steered for the shed, and I saw him pull a fist-sized cylindrical object from his jacket and raise it toward his mouth. The object looked a lot like a mountain bike handlebar grip with a metal ring attached to one end. Slim pulled the ring out with his teeth, and as he raced past the shed, he threw the cylinder through the doorway.

BOOM!

A deafening blast erupted from within the stone shed, accompanied by a brilliant flash of light through the doorway that made me see stars. The object was some kind of flash-bang stun grenade.

I blinked several times and turned back to the gap, where I saw movement. It was Hú Dié. She'd gotten her mountain bike and was fiddling with Trixie's quick-release seat post clamp. I took a step toward her but froze as Meathead reached the gap.

Hú Dié pulled the foot-long seat post out of Trixie's frame, the narrow racing seat still attached to one end of the post. She gripped the end of the post opposite the seat and hurled the whole thing like a tomahawk at Meathead's motorcycle. The rigid aluminum seat post caught in the heavy-duty spokes of the motorcycle's front wheel, then jammed up against the back of the front fork.

The front wheel locked up, and Meathead sailed over the handlebars, just as I had done when my mountain bike's front wheel tacoed, except Meathead was wearing a padded protective jacket and a fully enclosed helmet. The big man sailed into the compound, his head and shoulders skidding across the cobblestones as he hit the ground. The moment he came to rest, however, he stood up. His tinted face shield was scuffed and cracked, but otherwise he appeared fine. He tore off the damaged face shield, and I got a good look at his face. It was Meathead, without a doubt.

The engine on Meathead's riderless motorcycle cut out, and through the ringing in my ears I heard Slim's motorcycle engine rev. I looked over and saw that he was well past the shed and clear of the grenade's blast zone. However, his attention still seemed to be focused on the shed's doorway.

I glanced toward the building and saw Grandmaster Long stumble out of it. The old monk looked dazed and confused. He was staggering like a drunkard, his eyes a blank stare. He still held the dragon bone vessel tightly under one arm, and he now had a broadsword in his other hand.

Hú Dié let loose the same banshee wail she'd used when she'd attacked earlier, and I looked over to see her running full tilt toward Meathead. He was reaching across his body, into his riding jacket.

Hú Dié cocked her arm back as though about to throw a punch, and Meathead jerked his face to one side, out of her reach. However, the place where his face shield had been wasn't Hú Dié's target. Instead, she wound up with her entire torso and let fly the most wicked elbow I'd ever seen, connecting with the back of Meathead's hand, crushing it against his massive chest. I heard the thin bones in his hand snap and splinter like Popsicle sticks.

Meathead howled and dropped something to the cobblestones. It was a gun. Hú Dié bent over, scooping it up. She had nearly straightened when Meathead kicked like a football player punting a football. His foot knocked the pistol from her hand, sending the gun clear over the perimeter wall, while his shin connected with her chin.

Hú Dié hit the ground, possibly knocked out. I considered running to help her, but Meathead had already turned his attention to Grandmaster Long. The old monk still looked dazed, but he held tightly to the dragon bone as well as the broadsword.

I raced to his side well ahead of Meathead. I made a move to grab the container from Grandmaster Long before he accidentally dropped it, but the confused monk swung his broadsword the moment my hands touched the vessel. I ducked just in time to miss the deadly blow. The grenade must have temporarily blinded him. He didn't recognize me.

"Grandmaster Long!" I shouted. "It's me! Phoenix!"

Grandmaster Long must have also been deafened by the blast, because he continued to swing the broadsword.

I took several steps backward, out of range. As Meathead neared, I heard Slim's engine rev again. I looked over to see the motorcycle spring forward like a hungry jaguar. Slim reached into his jacket and pulled out another grenade, raising its metal ring to his teeth.

I dropped to the ground and curled into a ball, closing my eyes tight and covering my ears with my hands. I heard something hit the cobblestones behind me as Slim's motorcycle zoomed past and then—

BOOM!

A white-hot flash of unimaginable brightness washed

over me, together with a sonic pulse that punched at my kidneys and rattled the bones of my inner ear. Behind me, Grandmaster Long howled in pain, then fell silent. Meathead howled, too.

I opened my eyes and found the world awash with stars like I'd experienced after the first grenade, only a hundred times worse. My head throbbed, and I was so disoriented that I didn't know which way was up. I tried to rise to my knees but toppled over.

Through the ringing in my ears, I heard the whine of a motorcycle engine. The motocross bike swung around and stopped a few feet from Grandmaster Long. I saw that the old monk no longer held the broadsword. He was lying flat on his back, either out cold or dead. Both of his legs had been burned by the incendiary flash.

The dragon bone vessel lay smashed beside Slim's motorcycle. Slim removed a fabric drawstring bag from his jacket and quickly scooped up all that he could of the dragon bone. Once he'd finished, he tied the bag closed and rammed it back into his jacket.

I looked past Slim and saw Meathead staggering as though he were standing in a stiff breeze. He must have had his bell rung by the blast, too. Beyond Meathead, Hú Dié was getting to her knees.

Slim shouted something to Meathead, and I recognized his voice. These were definitely the same guys who had broken into our house. Meathead stumbled over to the revving motorcycle and climbed onto the back.

I'd never been so angry in my life. I had to do something.

I managed to rise to a squatting position, like a toad. As the motorcycle skittered past me with a squeal of rubber, I launched myself into the air. My plan was to slam into Slim's torso, knocking him off the bike, but Slim saw me coming and stuck out his leg.

Slim's foot collided with my shoulder. My forward momentum stopped, and I grabbed hold of Slim's ankle. He twisted the throttle, and I was jerked forward so hard I thought my arms were going to rip out of their sockets. But I wasn't about to let go. I began to roll like an alligator and felt the cuff of Slim's pant leg catch between the motorcycle's chain and its drive sprocket.

Fearing for my fingers, I let go. Slim's entire body shifted down and to the right as the revolving sprocket tugged his pant leg down and around; however, he didn't fall as most people would have. Instead, he seemed to know exactly what to do. He kicked his leg out and then forward, tearing his pant leg up the back from ankle to knee. The slackened fabric spun out of the sprocket teeth, and Slim was free.

I stared. Behind the flapping remains of his pant leg was one of the largest calf muscles I'd ever seen. Slim's leg was shaved, and it looked as if someone had replaced his calf with a softball. Bulging veins crisscrossing his calf even resembled softball stitching.

Hú Dié shrieked, and I spun around. She was standing now, pointing toward the motorcycle as it raced through the gap in the wall and disappeared into the trees.

"What?" I asked.

"That driver," she replied. "Do you know him?"

"Yeah, he and the big guy are the ones who broke into my house."

"No, no," Hú Dié said, shaking her head. "You already said that. I mean, do you know his name?"

"Of course not. Why?"

"Because *I* do. I would recognize that calf muscle anywhere. I have had a crush on those legs and the man they belong to for a long time. His name is Lin Tan, and he is a Chinese cyclocross racer. He recently moved to Europe to join a Belgian race team called Team Vanderhausen. 'V equals Victory.' Have you heard of them?"

16

I stared at Hú Dié in disbelief. I glanced across the stained cobblestones at Grandmaster Long, who was still lying in front of the stone shed. Then I looked back at Hú Dié.

Her eyes remained fixed in the direction the motorcycle had gone.

"That man rides for Team Vanderhausen?" I asked. "Are you sure?"

"Positive," she replied. "Calf muscles like that are unique, especially with those veins. That was Lin Tan. I am sure of it."

"Well, your crush just stole Grandmaster Long's dragon bone. He may have killed him, too."

Hú Dié turned toward the monk and gasped. We headed for Grandmaster Long.

I cursed as we knelt next to the old monk, trying hard not to look at his leg burns. I was ecstatic when he opened his eyes.

"Phoenix?" Grandmaster Long asked in a strained voice.

"Yes," I replied loudly. "I'm here. Can you hear me?"

Grandmaster Long nodded. "I can hear you. My vision is returning, too. Those were stun grenades. Their effects are designed to be short-term."

"But your legs," Hú Dié said. "They are badly burned."

Grandmaster Long raised his head and peered down at the blistering skin on his shins. He smirked, laying his head back down. "I was an Iron Shin master in my younger days. The training destroyed most of the nerve endings below my knees. I hardly feel a thing. I will heal soon enough. Dragon bone will help."

"But it's gone," I said. "Those guys took it."

"All of it?" Hú Dié asked.

I motioned toward the remains of the shattered dragon bone vessel. "I might be able to sweep a few teaspoons' worth from the cracks in the cobblestones, but it will be dirty."

"Dirty is fine," Grandmaster Long said, "and two or three teaspoons will be sufficient. By the time I use it up, I will have healed enough to travel to another location, where I have more hidden. It is not a lifetime's worth, though. Phoenix, I am sorry. I will no longer be able to help your grandfather."

I lowered my head. "I understand. I apologize for the misfortune I have brought you."

"There is no need to apologize."

"But it's my fault," I said, looking up. "I don't know how, but they followed me. I think I know how to find them, though. I will get it back."

"You know who did this?"

"Hú Dié believes she recognized one of the men."

"It is Lin Tan," Hú Dié said. "I'm certain."

"Who is Lin Tan?" Grandmaster Long asked.

"A professional bicycle racer," I said.

"A cyclist?" Grandmaster Long said. "Hmm. In addition to its accelerative healing qualities, dragon bone also enhances physical performance. Perhaps the thieves have learned this."

"That's it!" I said. "Bicycle racing is crazy competitive. Like a lot of sports, multimillion-dollar contracts are at stake. Riders are always looking for an edge."

"They have no idea what they are dealing with," Grandmaster Long said. "Dragon bone is dangerous. What will you do next?"

"I'll figure something out. First, I need to use a telephone."

"There are no phones here."

"There is one at the shop," Hú Dié said.

"Then we have to get back there," I said. "Nice work stopping the big guy's motorcycle with your seat post, but do you think you can still ride Trixie?"

Hú Dié shook her head. "No way. My seat post has to be trashed. I can't ride all the way back to Kaifeng without one, and we can't both ride your bike. We might be able to take the motorcycle, though."

"Do you think you can fix it?" I asked. "Do you even know how to drive one?"

Hú Dié looked offended. "If it's made of metal, I can fix it. If it has two wheels, I can ride it."

"You rock," I said, and turned to Grandmaster Long. "Is there anything we can do for you?"

"No," Grandmaster Long replied. "I will be fine." As if to prove his point, he stood. He wobbled a bit, his legs looking as though they might give out any second, but then he steadied himself. "I have been in far worse condition, Phoenix," he said. "So has your grandfather. When I lost my eyesight from that flash grenade, all I could think about was him."

"Why?"

Grandmaster Long sighed. "You do not know this tale, either?"

"Grandfather told me that he once knew a boy who lost his eyesight, but the boy's vision returned after using dragon bone. That boy was Grandfather?"

"Why don't you ask him?" Grandmaster Long said. "We have work to do. I will get something to put the dragon bone in. You two, fix that motorcycle." He turned and slowly began to walk toward the inner compound.

Hú Dié was already heading to Meathead's motorcycle. "Go get the backpack," she called.

I retrieved the hydration pack from my bike and went over to where she was kneeling beside the motorcycle. She had pulled Trixie's seat post from the spokes of the motorcycle's front wheel. The aluminum bicycle seat post was bent and cracked. It was useless. The motorcycle spokes, however, didn't look too bad. Two were broken, and one was bent, but the rest of them and the front fork appeared to be fine.

"Maybe we're in luck," Hú Dié said. "Find my multi-tool. It kind of looks like an oversized Swiss Army knife."

"I know what a multi-tool is," I said, digging through the pack. I found the device and slapped it into Hú Dié's waiting palm like an operating room nurse handing a clamp to a surgeon. She unfolded the multi-tool's pliers and used them to twist the two broken spokes around the two nearest undamaged ones. Then she began to tap each of the remaining spokes, one at a time, with the pliers.

"What are you doing?" I asked.

"Hush!" she replied. She continued tapping, lightly striking each spoke in sequence around the entire wheel. I noticed that the spokes all rang out at more or less the same pitch, which probably meant they were all under the same amount of tension. This was good. Hú Dié tapped the bent spoke last; I heard what sounded like a dull thump.

She turned to me. "I think we can ride it. The spokes sound like they are all tightened about the same amount, except for the bent one, but there is no point in trying to straighten it. If I accidentally break it, we're done. Three broken spokes is one too many. Help me stand her up. I need to check one more thing."

I helped Hú Dié muscle the motorcycle onto its wheels, and I grunted with the effort. It had to weigh close to three hundred pounds.

"This thing is heavy," I said.

"Heavy is good," she said. "It means there is a lot of

gas." She removed the gas cap and peered into the tank. Hú Dié smiled.

"We really are in luck," she said, replacing the cap. "This bike has an oversized gas tank for long-distance riding, and the tank is nearly full. Most motocross motorcycle tanks hold less than two gallons, which would only get us fifty miles, maximum. This one holds almost double that. We should be able to make it all the way home without refueling. It also has passenger foot pegs welded on."

I noticed there was a bungee net strung over the back section of the seat, holding down a small folded blanket. "What's this?"

"I don't know," Hú Dié replied, "but you're going to have to get rid of it. Otherwise, you'll have nowhere to sit."

I unhitched the springy cargo net and grabbed the blanket. There was something wrapped inside. I flipped back the top fold and saw a brand-new notebook computer. Promotional stickers were still affixed to its outer casing, touting the machine's high-end capabilities. I opened the lid and it woke from sleep mode.

My blood ran cold.

Hú Dié looked at me. "A computer? That's interesting. What's wrong? You don't look so good."

"I know how those guys found us," I said. "This computer is running GPS software. I believe it was used to program *my* GPS unit. They must have stolen the computer from my grandfather's friend PawPaw. She told me that she just bought a new notebook." I minimized the GPS software window and saw that the computer's wallpaper was a photo of a Chinese apothecary shop. "This was PawPaw's, for sure. I have to get to a phone as quickly as possible."

"Let's leave now. Go get our helmets. I'll try to start the motorcycle."

"What about the backpack?"

"Leave it. I don't want to risk you on the back with all that extra weight tossing you around. I'll return sometime and get it, along with Trixie. I can't abandon her. We should probably leave the computer, too, unless you think we'll need it. It will be too difficult to carry."

"We don't need it." I pulled my passport and wallet out of the pack and shoved them into one of my cargo shorts' zippered pockets. Then I clamped the computer under my arm and retrieved our bike helmets as Hú Dié climbed onto the motorcycle and fired it up, working the kick-starter, clutch, and throttle like a pro. The dirt bike sounded fine.

I strapped on my helmet and looked back toward the stone shed. Grandmaster Long had returned with a small Chinese teacup, a piece of rice paper, and an old-fashioned Chinese calligraphy paintbrush. He was lying on the cobblestones, brushing dragon bone from the cracks onto the paper, then pouring the dragon bone into the teacup.

I jogged over to him and set the computer next to the teacup. "Do you think you will see PawPaw soon?"

"I was just thinking about arranging a meeting with her," he replied. "Why?"

"Could you please give this to her? And could you also keep our pack and bikes until we can figure out a way to get them back?"

"Of course. The computer belongs to PawPaw?"

"I'm pretty sure, yeah. She said she bought a new notebook computer to program the GPS unit that she loaned me in order to find you."

"You think those men stole it from her?"

"Yes. Those guys probably bugged our phone in Indiana or placed a listening device in our house or something. Then they would have known that I was going to see her before coming here. I'm so stupid for not thinking of it sooner. I'm worried about her."

"Did those men harm you or your grandfather?"

"Not really."

"Then it is very likely that PawPaw is safe. They don't sound like killers. They may have stolen whatever dragon bone she had readily available, but even that would likely be an insubstantial amount. PawPaw is the most careful of the three of us."

"I still plan to call her when we get back to Kaifeng. I don't care if someone has bugged her phone. I need to make sure she is okay."

"Then you had better get moving. She goes to bed early and sleeps like the dead. It is a side effect of the dragon bone. She won't hear your call."

"I know," I replied. "Grandfather is the same way." I

bowed. "Thank you for everything, Grandmaster Long. I hope to see you again soon and return your dragon bone."

Grandmaster Long nodded. "Visit me regardless of what happens with the dragon bone. I still have many stories to share. Best of luck to you. I fear you are going to need it." He waved to Hú Dié, and she waved back, revving the engine.

I bowed one more time and then ran to Hú Dié. I handed her bicycle helmet to her, and she strapped it on as I climbed onto the seat behind her. There was very little room, and the firm, rectangular seat was uncomfortable. It got worse when I raised my feet onto the passenger foot pegs and found that my knees were nearly even with my chin. I was beginning to wonder what I should do with my hands when Hú Dié turned to me.

"You know how you often see women riding as passengers on motorcycles, and they have their arms wrapped loosely around the driver's waist?" she asked.

I swallowed hard. "Yes."

"Well, those women are idiots. Motorcycles designed for two people have handles. That's where you hold on. This motorcycle wasn't originally designed for two, but someone added those foot pegs and oversized bungee net tie-downs, which also serve as handles. Use them. The other option would be for you to latch tightly on to me like that big guy did with Lin Tan. Try that, and you'll find yourself eating one of my elbows."

17

I gripped the handles on the motorcycle seat with all my might as I stared over Hú Dié's shoulder. We powered through the late afternoon sun out of the Cangzhen compound and onto the forest trail I had blazed with my bike. I found myself transfixed.

The world came at me so fast, it felt as if we were time traveling. Trees and ferns zipped past at a tremendous rate, forming permanent green and brown streaks in the periphery of my vision. It was similar to ripping through the undergrowth down a steep slope while atop a mountain bike, only this was much more stable and way faster. Hú Dié kept the handlebars rigidly on track, and I had a sense that she was riding at the very limit of her capabilities. It worried me, but at the same time, it added to the thrill.

My initial rush and excitement about riding on the powerful machine wore off once we broke out of the trees and began to climb our first slope. From there on out, it was work. I had to continuously adjust my balance in relation to Hú Dié's, whether we were going up a mountainside or coming back down.

When we finally left the mountain trail and entered the village with the well, I was glad to see no sign of the two guys who had tried to steal the GPS. It was dinnertime, and the streets were mostly empty. We passed through there in minutes.

With the foothills behind us, I found that I had an even bigger challenge ahead. I needed to stay awake over all the flat, wearisome pavement before us. Being on the back was *boring*.

By the time we reached the outskirts of Kaifeng, I was ready to peel myself off the vinyl-covered seat and swear an oath that I would never be a passenger on a motorcycle again. Thankfully, Hú Dié wove through the city traffic even faster than I thought possible, and we arrived back at the shop with half an hour of sunlight to spare. PawPaw should still be awake.

Hú Dié parked the motorcycle in the bike shop's loading bay, and we went inside, where she led me to a telephone. Next to the phone was a box of rags, and she tossed several to me. We removed our bicycle helmets and shoes, wiping sweat and grime off our faces, arms, and legs.

When we had finished, Hú Dié asked, "Do you know your grandfather's friend's telephone number?"

"Yes."

"All right. I am going upstairs to see if my father is

home. I'll be down in a few minutes. I'll see if I can find us something to eat, too."

I nodded, then dialed the number while Hú Dié headed upstairs. PawPaw answered on the second ring.

"Hello?"

The familiar voice sent a wave of relief surging through me. "PawPaw! It's me, Phoenix. I just had a run-in with the dragon bone thieves from Indiana. Are you okay?"

"Phoenix! Dear me. Those two bullies broke in here last night right after I went to bed. I'm fine, how are you?"

"I'm okay. Tell me what happened. How did you know it was the same guys I'm talking about?"

"Your grandfather told me what they look like. The big one made me sit still at gunpoint while the other one tore my apartment apart until he found my dragon bone. I have more stashed away, of course, so I am perfectly fine. How are *you*?"

"Physically, I'm all right. Mentally, I've never been angrier. I think they bugged Grandfather's phone and learned about you. I feel so stupid that I didn't see it coming. They stole your new computer, didn't they?"

"Yes, and I've been worried sick about you ever since, because they could figure out where you were going. I am so relieved that you called. Don't feel stupid. You had no way of knowing. This morning, I bought a few new gadgets from an electronics store and found that some-one had tapped my landline telephone. My equipment told me that a listening device was still connected to your grandfather's phone, too. Needless to say, I've taken care of the issues with my phone. We can speak openly now. What happened with you?"

I filled her in on everything, including Hú Dié.

"Phoenix," she said, "I told you not to talk with strangers, especially in Kaifeng."

"I know, but she's helped me like you wouldn't believe. Ask Grandmaster Long. He'll tell you. He knows of her family. Their last name is Tiě. Her first name is Hú Dié."

PawPaw hesitated. "I am sure Long does know of them. Your grandfather, however, does not. Be careful, Phoenix."

"What do you mean? Do you know the family?"

"I've never met them, but there are rumors—clues as to what kind of people they may be."

I lowered my voice. "They're cheats, if you ask me. At least in their business."

"So, you know what they do for a living?"

"Yeah, I'm in the back of their shop right now. I sort of stumbled across the truth."

"How do you feel about what they do?"

"I don't like it."

"And how do you think this Hú Dié feels about her family's line of work?"

"She doesn't see anything wrong with it. She says they're honest with their customers, and it is actually their customers who are the cheats. It's all so confusing."

"Do you trust her?"

"I trust her with my life. She put her own life on the

line for me—twice. Grandmaster Long trusts her, too. He even showed her the dragon bone."

"Oh, dear," PawPaw said.

"Don't worry," I said. "Hú Dié can keep a secret. Grandmaster Long even thinks so."

"Just keep your eyes and ears open, Phoenix. Get back to Beijing as soon as you can."

"I will. Have you heard from Grandfather? I was planning to call him, but it's still a little early back home. He was sleeping in very late right before I left."

"We spoke earlier, after I wiped my phone line clean. He is in the nursing home."

"What? Already?"

"I am afraid so. It's not all bad, though. This is more a precautionary measure. Your uncle Tí has him in a private room, and no one else knows that he is there. Your uncle is going to purchase a pay-as-you-go international cellular phone for your grandfather, and he is supposed to call me in the morning to test it out. You should probably wait until you have that phone number before you try calling him, just to be safe. When should I tell him to arrange your return flight?"

"I don't know yet. I may be going to Texas."

"Texas! Whatever for?"

"I might know the identity of one of the thieves— the slim one. He's a cyclist, and he now rides for a team whose owner asked me to ride with them this summer at their new training facility. Please tell Grandfather that I will probably accept the offer. Let him know why, too. I don't want him to think that I'm abandoning him."

"Phoenix, this is too much. You should notify American authorities. Let them deal with it."

"No. Grandfather didn't want to get the police involved. You know how he is about answering questions. We need to keep dragon bone a secret. I want to give this a try myself. I've heard a few things about a group of kids called the Five Ancestors. Grandmaster Long said I am the last of their line. They were all roughly my age when they supposedly saved China like three hundred fifty years ago. All *I* want to do is save my grandfather."

"Oh, Phoenix. You have no idea what you are saying."

"Sorry, I've made up my mind."

PawPaw sighed. "Then there is no more to say. If you are half as stubborn as your grandfather, there is no point in my trying to argue. Let me know as soon as possible what your plans are. I want to keep your grandfather up to date, and I want to check on Long."

"Will do," I replied, "and thank you."

"Save the thank-yous for later. Just be safe, and stay in touch. Goodbye, Phoenix."

"Goodbye, PawPaw."

I hung up the phone and wondered, *Do I really want to do this?*

Yes, I decided. *I do.*

I heard a muffled crash upstairs, followed by the sound of pounding feet. I ran to the base of the stairs and saw a closed door overhead. Two people were arguing behind it. The door burst open, and Hú Dié stormed through, shouting back over her shoulder in a Chinese dialect that I didn't understand. A man's voice began to shout back, but she slammed the door closed, cutting him off in midsentence. She stomped down the stairs.

"*Fathers,*" she said in English, rolling her eyes. She handed me a bottle of water and a sandwich.

"Thanks," I said, taking a bite. "Is everything okay?"

"Of course. We just had a small disagreement."

"Small?"

"Yes."

"About what?"

"Family stuff."

"What was that crash, then?"

Hú Dié rubbed her forearms. "My father decided to stop listening to me, and he turned up the volume on his television. He will be shopping for a new one as soon as he can afford it."

"Um, okay."

Hú Dié nodded toward the opposite side of the room. "I want to show you something."

I followed her to a cluttered workbench. She grabbed a milk crate filled with cycling magazines and began to rummage through them. They were all in English, and every type of cycling seemed to be represented, from mountain biking to downhill racing, to road racing, to cyclocross, to BMX, to free riding. She selected one called *Cyclocross Magazine* and began to flip through it.

"Reading these is one of the ways I work on my English," she said. She stopped flipping and pointed to a page. "Here! See? I told you."

I glanced over her shoulder and saw a half-page advertisement. The main focus of the ad was a photograph of a cyclocross rider on his bike, traveling away from the camera, hammering hard. His shaved calf muscle bulged like an alien appendage, complete with a unique pattern of thick, wriggling veins. That definitely looked like the leg I had seen at Cangzhen.

In addition to the photo, the ad contained two lines of text:

I got my backpack from home and rummaged around in one of the pockets until I found Dr. V's business card. I'd brought it with me as a reminder of what was waiting for me back in Indiana after this mess was over. Even though I wasn't interested in racing for Dr. V, it was still nice to know that I was invited to ride with a real team. It also reminded me that I had several races left this summer with Jake.

I grabbed the telephone and checked my watch. It would be early in Texas, but it was still worth a try. "May I borrow your phone again?"

Hú Dié looked at the logo on the business card. "Is this a joke?"

"No."

"What are you going to do, call Team Vanderhausen and ask for Lin Tan?"

"Can I use your phone or not? It's an international call."

Hú Dié gave me an exasperated look. "Be my guest, but you are going to let me listen in if the call gets interesting."

"Suit yourself." I dialed the number on the card, and it rang several times. I was about to hang up, when someone answered.

"Team Vanderhausen. May I help you?" It was a woman's voice.

"Hi," I said. "Is Dr. Vanderhausen available?"

"Not currently. If you would like to leave a message, someone will get back to you."

"It's kind of important," I said. "I really need to talk with him. Can you please tell him it's Phoenix Collins? He gave me his card."

"Is that your real name? *Phoenix?*"

"Yes, ma'am."

"Are you an acquaintance of his?"

"He invited me to train with his team this summer."

Hú Dié punched me in the arm. She placed her ear next to the receiver.

The woman on the other end of the telephone line said, "You sound a little young."

"I'm thirteen," I replied. "I race against his nephew, Ryan."

"Where are you calling from? I don't recognize this extension."

"China."

"China? Isn't it the middle of the night there?"

"Almost. That's why I'm calling now."

The woman sighed. "Hold, please. I'll try his cell phone."

I heard a click, and elevator music began to play. Hú Dié pulled away.

"Were you really invited to ride with them?" she asked.

"Yes."

"When?"

"Right before I came here."

"How come you never told me?"

"I don't know," I said.

"So, are you going to do it?"

"I'm not sure."

"What do you mean, you're not sure? I would *kill* for a chance to—"

The elevator music cut out, and I held my hand up. "Shut up and ride," I whispered.

Hú Dié pouted and cocked her arm as if to hit me again, but then she lowered her fist and pressed her ear back to the receiver.

There was a click on the other end of the telephone line, and I heard Dr. V's accented voice. "Phoenix?"

"Hi, Dr. V," I said, trying to sound casual. "I'm sorry to interrupt your day."

"No, no. I finished my morning ride more than an hour ago. It's so infernally hot here in Texas, I like to try to get off the road before the sun comes up. Early to bed, early to rise, makes a man healthy, wealthy . . . and all that. Did I hear correctly that you are in China?"

I had been thinking about how to answer this question ever since we had left Cangzhen Temple. "Yes," I said, "I'm visiting relatives. That's why I felt I couldn't take you up on your offer to ride. Sorry if I was rude. I think I made some kind of sarcastic remark about Texas being too hot in June."

"Well, you were right about the heat. What can I do for you?"

"To be honest, I've been here a few days and I'm bored out of my mind. My grandfather is on his way, but I don't see this trip getting any better."

"But you're halfway around the world. Isn't it exciting? A foreign country with unique culture and exotic food and—"

"They dry their rice on oil-stained asphalt," I said. "I'd rather be riding my bike."

Dr. V burst into laughter. "You'd rather be riding your bike than vacationing? That is *exactly* the kind of thing I want to hear from my riders! Have you discussed this with your grandfather?"

"Yes," I lied. "He is disappointed that I would rather be in Texas than China, but he said I could go if it wouldn't cost him anything."

"Don't worry about the cost, as I've already told you. You won't even have to use your return plane ticket. It will be easier if my travel agent handles everything from scratch. Our team attorney can make sure that your travel documentation is in order, too. I've worked with riders from all over the world. We even have one guy from China. Did you know that?"

I paused. "No."

"His name is Lin Tan, but you won't get to meet him. He was suspended a month ago for using a banned growth hormone. He isn't allowed to ride with us again until next year."

"Really? That's too bad."

"It is. He's good. To make matters worse, my head of security was in on it. I had to let him go."

Head of security? That could easily be Meathead. My heart sank. Maybe Dr. V wasn't behind the dragon bone thefts after all. Perhaps Lin Tan and Meathead were working for someone else? Or maybe it was just the two of them after the dragon bone?

"So, how soon would you like to come?" Dr. V asked.

I didn't answer. My mind was still racing.

Hú Dié jabbed an elbow in my side. She moved her mouth to my other ear and whispered, "He's lying about something. I can tell. You have to go."

"Phoenix?" Dr. V said.

"Sorry," I replied. "The phone cut out for a second. I would like to come to Texas as soon as possible."

"That's great! I'm having an open house and a small cyclocross race with just our team members at the ranch a week from Saturday. I'd love for you to participate. The sooner you get here and get on a 'cross bike, the better. Where are you now, and what airport did you fly into?"

"I flew into Beijing International. Right now I'm in

the city of Kaifeng, a long bus ride south of Beijing, depending on farm traffic."

"Farm traffic? It sounds like you've had quite the adventure already. Stay right where you are. Give me twelve hours, and someone from my staff will call you back. The answering service has logged your telephone number, so I think we're good to go. If all goes well, you should be here in a couple days. Is there any chance your grandfather can accompany you?"

"Er . . . no. He's not even here yet. Why?"

"I am willing to bet there are no direct flights from Beijing to Austin, Texas. That means you will have to enter the United States in a different city, and as a minor you will need an adult to either travel with you or meet you at the airport. Do you have any relatives in New York or Los Angeles? I know there are direct flights from Beijing to those cities."

I frowned. "No."

"What about adult relatives in China who would like a free trip to the United States? Perhaps a cousin? The person only needs to be eighteen years old."

Hú Dié began to jump up and down. She whispered in my ear again. "Tell him yes! Tell him yes!"

I scratched my head. "Um, I think so," I said into the telephone. "I'll have to ask, though."

"Great!" Dr. V said. "When you find somebody, you can give your temporary guardian's name to my travel agent when she calls you in the morning. As long as that person has a passport, we'll take care of the rest. I don't imagine that your relative will want to stay in our training facility, so we'll figure out something else. Perhaps a couple nights in Austin, then a week in Los Angeles or New York. I will pick up the cost for everything, of course."

"That is very generous."

"What is the point of having money if you don't get to spend it? I have a cyclocross team, but I bought Ryan a twelve-thousand-dollar mountain bike to ride at a single race in Indiana. The least I can do is spend a few thousand dollars to get you here. From what I understand, you make Ryan look like a tortoise, and he's no slouch. I enjoy spoiling my riders and their families. I should probably get off the phone now and get started on this. Do you have any questions?"

"No, sir," I said. "Thank you very much."

"Thank *you*, Phoenix. I'll see you at the ranch. Bye."

"Goodbye."

Dr. V hung up.

"Woo-hoo!" Hú Dié shouted. "Is the ranch near Austin?"

I hung up the phone and looked at her. "Yeah, why?"

"Austin is where Lance Armstrong lives! He even has a bike shop downtown! I've always wanted to go there!"

"You think *you're* going to be my guardian? I assumed you had a cousin you could loan me."

"No way. I wouldn't miss this for the world."

"But you're only fourteen."

"Says who? Let me show you something."

Hú Dié headed over to the counter that separated the shop's retail space from the fabrication area. She cleared everything off the countertop, then took hold of one end. "Grab the other end," she said. "Help me lift it off. It's not attached."

I helped her, and we set the countertop on the floor. The counter's base was hollow. Inside was a long, narrow machine unlike any I'd ever seen. "What is it?" I asked.

"A printing press," Hú Dié said proudly. "It's an antique. I carve custom printing plates for it out of metal."

I remembered what Grandmaster Long said about Hú Dié's shop selling more than bikes, and PawPaw's questions and comments about her family. My face turned to stone.

"You forge passports as well as bikes?" I said. "That's nothing to be proud of."

"Do you want to go to Texas or not?"

I ground my teeth. "Yes."

"Then stop being so righteous. What was it you said earlier? Oh, yeah—*shut up and ride.*"

STAGE THREE

FINAL RULE OF CYCLING
To Finish First, You Must First Finish

Hú Dié's passport-forging skills seemed to be as good as her bike-forging skills. A day and a half after calling Dr. V, I found myself sitting ten rows behind "Cousin" Hú Dié on a flight to Austin, Texas. She certainly knew how to get her way. She even had a better seat than I did.

After getting our travel papers from Dr. V's people, we began our journey with an hour-long bus ride from the station in Kaifeng to the city of Zhengzhou. From Zhengzhou we flew to Beijing, and from Beijing we flew to Los Angeles, crossing over the international date line and screwing up my sense of day and night once more. Now we were headed to Austin, but it was just a few hours on the local clock after we'd left China. It was all so confusing.

At least having Hú Dié act as my legal guardian made sense. U.S. Customs had been a breeze when we arrived in Los Angeles, and there should be no reason anyone in

Austin would question us, as this was a domestic flight. I hated to admit it, but it was a good idea having her come along.

The official plan was for Hú Dié to go all the way to the ranch with me for a quick tour; then she would be driven to Austin, where she would spend some time. From there, she was to fly to Los Angeles for a week before heading back to China. Unofficially, however, she and I were planning to do everything possible to have her remain at the ranch. Our goal was to persuade Dr. V to bring her onto the team as an unpaid mechanic's apprentice for her ninety-day travel visa. She would work on the team's cutting-edge bikes until we could run off with the dragon bone.

If the dragon bone wasn't there, I planned to head back to Indiana as soon as possible. Hú Dié could stay with the team if she was having a good time. After seeing Hú Dié in action the past few days, I had no doubt that she would weasel her way onto Team Vanderhausen.

I glanced up the aisle at her, still finding it difficult to believe that it was really Hú Dié. Before we left, she'd put on makeup and styled her hair forward so that it hid most of her face. Delicate white gloves covered her grease-stained fingers, and her toenails were painted. She wore heeled sandals and a summer dress that made her look like a well-to-do young woman traveling on holiday. She easily looked the eighteen years her passport claimed, and no one challenged her.

Additionally, as we traveled through China, Hú Dié had spoken with firm authority, bossing ticket takers and flight attendants around so much that they left her alone. Now that we were in the United States, she'd gone completely silent, acting as if she knew no English and flashing her brilliant smile every five seconds. People left her alone now, too, but they did so with a polite courtesy that made me want to scream. If they only knew what she was really like.

Before leaving China, I told Hú Dié about Ryan and Jake. I was bothered by the way Ryan had acted toward me the last time I saw him, but she told me to get over it. She said I couldn't change someone's behavior; only they could change it, so worrying about *why* someone changed was pointless. All I could do was accept things as they were now and move forward. In some ways, she sounded like Grandfather.

I closed my eyes and leaned back in my seat. I couldn't stop thinking about Grandfather. I had spoken with him twice, and he'd insisted he was fine. He claimed he'd moved into the nursing home only as a precaution. However, I also spoke with my uncle, who told me a different story. Grandfather had attempted to decrease the amount of dragon bone he took each day in order to make his tiny supply last longer, but his body wasn't handling it well. Uncle Tí had been frantically searching for potential treatments for Grandfather, but so far he'd found nothing.

I hoped I was doing the right thing in flying to Austin. If Dr. V wasn't involved in this, I would be wasting a huge amount of time. However, while Dr. V had never given me a reason to distrust him, Hú Dié had said she could tell by his voice when she had listened in earlier that he had been lying or at least misleading me. If anyone knew about misleading people, it was Hú Dié. Maybe Dr. V was behind it, after all. Either way, Hú Dié and I would have to be very careful around him, and assume he knew exactly why I'd suddenly changed my mind and decided to join him at the ranch.

I ran my hands through my hair. As I drifted off to sleep, I thought regardless of Dr. V's guilt or innocence, if Grandfather were to slip away without my having said goodbye, I would hate myself forever.

I woke when the plane touched down in Austin. I checked my watch. It was 11:30 a.m. local time on Saturday—one full week since Lin Tan and Meathead had broken into our home. Time was going by so fast.

Hú Dié and I departed the plane and headed to the baggage claim. As we approached it, I saw a tall, wiry man wearing jeans and a T-shirt, along with scuffed cowboy boots and a straw cowboy hat. His leathery face was nearly as creased as PawPaw's, though he was probably only forty years old. He held a small sign that read TEAM VANDERHAUSEN.

I turned to Hú Dié. "That's us."

She didn't reply. She just smiled. Apparently, she was still deep into her role of "pretty but linguistically challenged young Chinese woman." I fought the urge to punch her in the arm and looked back at the guy with the sign.

"Phoenix and his cousin?" the man drawled in a Southern accent.

I nodded.

"Name's Murphy," he said. "I work for Dr. V. Y'all come with me."

We retrieved our luggage. I had my backpack and carry-on duffel bag, while Hú Dié had two large suitcases plus a carry-on. I didn't know what she had in the suitcases, but judging by the extra fees billed to the team for those bags being too heavy, it wouldn't surprise me if it was tools. Murphy helped her, and though he was thin, he was strong as a mule. He didn't even flinch under the weight of the bags.

We walked outside, stepping into a wall of dry Texas heat. I was wearing a T-shirt and cargo shorts, and my arms, legs, and face suddenly felt as if I'd leaned too close to a campfire. How could anyone live here?

Murphy led us to a large black SUV parked in the garage across the street, and Hú Dié and I climbed into the backseat. I was already soaked with sweat. Murphy loaded our luggage into the back, grunting softly under the weight of Hú Dié's suitcases, and he climbed into the driver's seat. He sent a short text message with his cell phone, and then we pulled out of the airport.

The city of Austin was in the distance, and Hú Dié stared longingly out the tinted rear windows as though willing the vehicle to exit the highway and head toward the skyscrapers downtown and the famous bike shop in their shadows. That didn't happen.

We headed west, and I watched as the landscape changed from typical American cityscape to something out of a surreal movie. Concrete gave way to parched, cracked soil and sagebrush, and the surrounding flatlands rose steadily in the distance. We were about to enter the famous Texas Hill Country.

As we passed over the first hill, civilization thinned, replaced by thousand-acre ranches bordered by miles of nearly invisible barbed-wire fencing. The hills ebbed and flowed around us in smooth arcs. Sparse patches of thorny bushes and stubby trees dotted the landscape, connected by alternating fields of huge boulders and dry, stunted grass. My pulse began to quicken. The farther we went, the more excited I felt. Despite the heat, I realized I would give almost anything for a chance to rip through those hilly fields on a mountain bike. As much as I hated the thought, I might have to break down and ask permission to borrow Ryan's.

About twenty minutes later, we veered southwest. The outside temperature gauge on the dashboard read ninety-nine degrees Fahrenheit.

The SUV stopped abruptly before a gated ranch road that looked like all the other gated ranch roads we had passed. Murphy got out and punched a code into a keypad, and the gate opened.

I leaned over to Hú Dié and whispered, "Did you get the digits?"

"No," she replied. "His body was blocking the keypad."

"I couldn't see it, either," I said. "Too bad."

Murphy got back in and pulled through the gate,

which closed behind us. We drove over a hilly, winding dirt road for quite a while before I saw what had to be the training facility.

The building stood alone. There wasn't a tree or bush within five hundred yards. It was a single-story structure about three times the size of Hú Dié's bike shop and was built of tan cinder blocks. A rectangle with a flat roof, the building had just a few windows that I could see, and all were made of smoked glass. I only saw one door.

It didn't look like any training facility I'd ever imagined. It looked like a miniature prison.

The driveway ended in a large parking lot, part of which was covered with a metal roof. There was room for several dozen vehicles under there, but I saw only three. One was a battered old full-sized pickup truck. One was a black SUV like the one we were in, and the last was a large touring motorcycle with a huge windshield, a gigantic dashboard, rigid saddlebags, and an Indiana license plate. I guessed that the SUV belonged to the team, while the pickup belonged to Murphy. As for the motorcycle, I had seen it before. It used to belong to Ryan's father. Dr. V must have gotten it from Ryan's mother.

There was one other item in the parking lot. It was a combination RV/horse trailer. The front half was a camper, while the back was basically a mobile barn with room for a couple of horses and their associated tack. These were a common sight in the horse-friendly state-park campgrounds that Grandfather and I sometimes visited in Indiana. My favorite trails were categorized as nonmotorized multi-use, which meant that hikers, mountain bikers, and horseback riders all frequented them. I'd ridden through so much horse dung, I considered myself an honorary cowboy.

Murphy parked the SUV in the shade of the carport, and we all climbed out. I heard the buzz of a large fan from inside the horse trailer, and the hum of an air conditioner atop the camper. There was a long power cord running from the camper to the building. I glanced back at the trailer and saw the swish of a horse's black tail between the trailer's aluminum slats.

"Ain't but one horse in there," Murphy said. "Name's Theo. I suggest you leave him be. That tin can's been our home for six months straight. Made him skittish as all get-out."

Hú Dié looked at him. "You've lived here half a year? Why?"

Murphy grinned. "I wasn't sure you could speak English, young lady, though Dr. V heard from the travel agent that you could speak it very well. I've been overseeing this here building construction."

"It looks finished to me," I said.

"Contractors are out, but I've got a few more finishing touches to take care of inside before Thursday."

"What happens Thursday?" Hú Dié asked.

"Rest of the team arrives," Murphy replied.

I looked at all the empty covered parking spaces. "So, who's here now?"

"Just Dr. V and Ryan."

"Until Thursday?"

"Yep."

I was liking the sound of this more and more. Fewer people would make the job of snooping around for the dragon bone easier.

Hú Dié fanned herself with one hand. "It is sooo hot out here. Why did you bring your horse?"

"Dr. V also hired me to build him a cyclocross course that he laid out," Murphy said. "The trail is a mile and a half long and the regulation three meters wide. That's a lot of ground to beat down. I rode Theo over it every morning and evening for five months, rain or shine. He's a big quarter horse. Weighs near thirteen hundred pounds. Got the job done a month ahead of schedule."

I raised an eyebrow. "Good idea. I've seen what horses can do to a trail."

Murphy nodded. "Ain't nothing gonna grow on that course for years."

"Can we see the course?" Hú Dié asked.

"Sure enough," Murphy said.

"Wait," I said. "Can we see it some other time? I'm exhausted."

"It's in your best interest if I show you the course now," Murphy said. "Trust me on that."

I frowned, trying to figure out what he meant, when Hú Dié suddenly squealed, "Oh, look, Phoenix! He's so cute!"

I turned toward her, expecting to see Theo's nose poking out between the trailer slats. Instead, I saw the head of a large, friendly-looking dog in one of the camper windows. I'd never seen one like it before. Its coat was short and tan-colored, and its muzzle was black. It had medium-sized floppy ears and a thick neck, but its face was long and narrow, and its nose was huge. It was as if a mastiff had been crossed with some kind of hound. The dog's lazy eyes appeared to be smiling, and its tongue lolled happily out of its mouth over bulging jaw muscles.

Hú Dié looked at Murphy. "Is he nice?"

"Sweet as pie."

Hú Dié stepped up to the window, and the dog leaned toward her. She placed her hand on the glass, and the dog went ballistic. It curled its lips back into a vicious snarl, slamming its face into the window. It growled savagely, working its massive jaws up and down against the glass. Saliva ran down the window like rain.

Hú Dié jumped back, and the dog stopped as though someone had flipped a switch. It pulled away from the window, its tongue flopping back out and its eyes as happy and lazy as ever.

"You call that *sweet*!" Hú Dié shouted. "What kind of pie do you serve here in Texas?"

Murphy chuckled. "Keep your hands off me and my property, and that dog will love you all day long. Do me wrong, and beware. A couple years ago, a man broke into my trailer. Both his arms and one leg were all kinds of broke before I pulled old Bones off him."

I cringed. "Bones? Is that his name?"

"Yep. Ain't seen a bone yet that that dog can't snap with a single chomp. He's a black mouth cur. A huntin' dog. Best nose in the county and strongest jaws in the state, I'd wager."

"I think I've seen enough," Hú Dié said. "Can we please go to the cyclocross course now?"

"Yes, ma'am."

Hú Dié and I followed Murphy out of the carport. We walked behind the training facility, and I saw a treeless field that was flat compared with the surrounding area. A wide, winding cyclocross course had been pounded into the low, dry grass and was interspersed with man-made obstacles that made me begin to wonder what on earth I was doing here. I'd never ridden a course like this before.

I turned to Murphy. "Are you sure this can't wait?"

"Stop being such a sissy," Hú Dié said. "Give us the details, please, Mr. Murphy."

Murphy nodded. "Dr. V designed it. I didn't know the first thing about bike racing before this. My specialty is constructing buildings, but Dr. V seems happy enough with the course. It's a loop. There's the start/finish line." He pointed to a deep line that had been gouged into the ground across the width of the course. "Eighty percent of each race will take place out here in the open, where folks can see the riders. The course snakes around quite a bit, which will give spectators plenty of places to stand to watch the action. Dr. V tells me that cyclocross isn't like mountain biking or road racing, where fans sit in one spot for hours, only to see their favorite rider zip past for two seconds. If I had a choice, I suppose I'd rather watch cyclocross. The other twenty percent of the course twists and turns through some thick scrub, trees, and hills out of sight before looping back here to the field and the obstacles I made. Let me show them to you."

We walked over to a long sand pit as wide as the course. A course-wide mud bog that was even longer followed it.

"Rules dictate that a race includes at least three different types of terrain," Murphy said. "This course is mostly compacted dirt. However, that sand pit is a hundred yards long, and the mud bog is two hundred yards long. I installed fifty sprinkler heads and set them to run every couple hours to keep it from drying out."

I recalled a saying I'd once heard: "If it ain't muddy, it ain't cyclocross." Whatever. Mud was much cooler in its natural form, on a mountain bike trail.

We walked past the sand and mud, and I saw three large pieces of solid wood that had been set on edge about twenty feet from one another.

"They call those hurdles," Murphy said. "Each is six-teen inches high and an inch wide, and they span the width of the course, per regulations. Riders usually get over 'em by climbing off their bikes, throwing their bikes over their shoulders, jumping over all the hurdles, then getting back onto their bikes to continue the race. Seems like a whole lot of work to me, but rules are rules. Got to have at least three hurdles."

Following the hurdles was the worst section of all. It was a pair of tall, wooden staircase towers connected by a long, narrow plank.

Murphy pointed to the structure. "Each course is

supposed to have a 'defining feature.' Ours is what I call the Wooden Tightrope. That plank is three feet wide, thirty feet long, and fifteen feet off the ground. A rider needs to get off his bike, carry the bike up the stairs, run across the platform, go down the other staircase, then get back onto the bike and keep riding. After that is the start/finish line."

I shook my head at the ridiculousness of it all and considered the course's overall length and layout. I knew cyclocross races were usually based on time as opposed to a predetermined number of laps, with the average time length being one hour. Racers did as many laps as they could as fast as possible, and when the lead racer began what would be his final lap to get to the one-hour mark, a signal was given so that all the racers knew this would be their last trip around the track. I figured I could crank out a lap here in ten minutes on my mountain bike, assuming twenty percent of the track was beyond the hills like Murphy said. If racers could do the same on a cyclocross bike, then that would give crowd members six chances to see their favorite rider trip over a hurdle, face-plant into the mud, or break his neck falling off the Wooden Tightrope.

Silly, not to mention dangerous.

"What do y'all think?" Murphy asked.

"It's beautiful!" Hú Dié exclaimed.

I shrugged. "I'll decide after I ride it."

Murphy looked at me and smirked. "That's fair. I'll get my answer soon enough."

"What do you mean?"

Murphy nodded toward the building.

I turned and looked at the back of the training facility. It was just like the front, except the single door on this side was about eight feet wide and eight feet tall. It was a roll-up loading bay door like the one at Hú Dié's shop. I heard a garage door opener begin to whir, and the door rose. Ryan and Dr. V were standing behind the door. They headed toward us.

Ryan was decked out in a black and green Team Vanderhausen racing kit—short-sleeve zip-up jersey with custom graphics, padded riding shorts, and matching socks. He wore fingerless riding gloves and a helmet, as well as mountain biking shoes, like most cyclocross riders. His jersey and riding shorts were skintight. His arms looked nearly as big as my legs, and his legs were as big as Civil War cannons. He was pushing a cyclocross bike, and streams of hateful energy shot out of his eyes like laser beams toward me.

I swallowed hard and looked at Dr. V.

Dr. V was wearing a Team Vanderhausen racing kit of his own and a huge smile. He, too, was pushing a cyclocross bike. However, the bike wasn't for him. It was sized for someone smaller—someone roughly my height.

"Phoenix!" Dr. V said. "So nice to see you. Ryan has been *dying* to show you his new playground. What do you say to a friendly welcome race?"

19

I glanced from Dr. V to Ryan and then to the cyclocross bikes they were pushing. I suddenly felt more exhausted than ever. I realized that while it was early afternoon, my body still thought I was back in China, where it was something like two a.m. *tomorrow*. Crossing the international date line really messed up a person's sleep patterns, and my naps on the multiple airplane flights hadn't seemed to help much.

I looked at Dr. V. "Sorry. I can't race right now. Too much jet lag. Besides, it's like a thousand degrees out here."

"A bit of exercise will do you good," Dr. V replied in a good-natured tone. "It will help your body adjust quicker to the time change. As for the heat, how about you only race a single lap? You can at least do that much, can't you? I'm eager to see what you are capable of doing.

Professional racers deal with the stress of travel on a weekly basis."

I looked at Ryan's riding gear. I didn't have any of my own yet. I'd given my clothing and shoe sizes to the travel agent to pass along before I'd left China, but my official team kit was going to take a couple of days to make, and even longer to ship. It was coming all the way from Italy. Dr. V demanded nothing but the best.

"I don't have anything to wear," I said. "I don't even have a helmet."

"We have plenty of gear," Dr. V replied, pointing to one of the walls. "Come in here and take a look. Bring your cousin, too. By the way, Ms. Hú Dié, I am Dr. V. Welcome."

Hú Dié flashed her brilliant smile. "Pleased to meet you, sir."

The four of us walked through the huge doorway, followed by Murphy. The space appeared to be a large workshop and storage area. There were no windows, but there were two doors. One opened into a small bathroom. The other was closed and presumably led elsewhere inside the building. Shelves lined two of the shop walls, and a long workbench stood along the other. Most of the shelves were filled, as was the workbench. There were bike components of every kind, as well as enough tools to repair an army of bicycles. One shelving unit was stacked floor to ceiling with brand-new helmets still in their packaging from the manufacturer.

"Most of our equipment is here, and the team will

arrive Thursday to get ready for the race one week from today," Dr. V explained.

I looked at the bike Dr. V had leaning against him. The clip-in pedals were similar to the ones I had on my mountain bike back home, only way more expensive.

I pointed to the pedals. "Got shoes?"

A look of embarrassment passed over Dr. V's face. "Actually, no. At least, not in your size. They were ordered along with your team clothing."

"No problem," Hú Dié interjected. "I can take care of it. Do you have any bailing wire?"

Dr. V, Ryan, Murphy, and I all turned to Hú Dié. I didn't like where this was going.

"I don't think it's worth the trouble," I said. "Let's race some other time."

"It's no trouble at all," Hú Dié said. "I'll make a set of cages similar to the ones you used in China, only without straps. They'll work fine. It will only take five minutes." She turned to Dr. V. "Where is your bailing wire?"

Dr. V glanced at the workbench overflowing with tools. "I don't believe we have any. I take it you are a cyclocross fan?"

"I'm more than a fan," Hú Dié said with a huff. "I'm a participant. What kind of cyclocross team doesn't have bailing wire? Duct tape and bailing wire hold the cyclocross world together! What do you plan to do during a race when a bike breaks?"

"Give the rider a new bike," Dr. V replied. "That's within the rules."

Hú Dié sighed. "That's what rich road bikers do. Cyclocross races have pits with mechanics who are there to fix things quickly. That's part of the excitement, seeing how clever the mechanics are. Don't you have a mechanic?"

"Of course we have a mechanic. He will be here Thursday, but I highly doubt he will be bringing *bailing wire* with him."

Hú Dié pursed her lips and turned to Murphy. "What about you?"

Murphy grinned. "Got a roll in my truck bed. Use it all the time with Theo around. How much you want?"

"Six feet."

"Be right back."

"Hang on," Hú Dié said. "I'm coming with you."

Hú Dié and Murphy left the building, and Dr. V turned to me. "Is she joking?" he asked.

I shook my head. "I'm afraid not."

"So you got to ride a bike in China, after all? With her?"

"A bit," I replied, trying to keep the nervousness out of my voice. I didn't want to slip and accidentally give away too much information. "She and her father, my . . . um, uncle, own a bike shop. That's where I called you from. My grandfather thought I might like staying with them. The thing is, they live in a pretty big city and the drivers there are insane. There is no place to ride."

"Didn't you enjoy hanging out at the shop?"

"I like to break bikes, not fix them."

Dr. V chuckled. "A boy after my own heart. Is Hú Dié any good with a wrench?"

"Watch."

"*I'll* watch her," Ryan said with a devious snicker. "She's hot."

I shot him the evil eye.

"Boys," Dr. V said. "Be nice. Now, you'll have to excuse me for a moment. Nature calls." He headed into the shop's bathroom.

I turned to Ryan. "What has gotten into you, man? You never used to be like this."

"What do you mean?"

"You're rude. You're disrespectful. You *attacked* me back in Indiana. I thought we were friends."

"Friends? Ha! Friends invite each other to their houses. Between you and me there was a one-way street. The same with Jake. You guys came over to my place, but I was never invited to either of yours."

I thought about it. He kind of had a point. "What about your dad's, uh . . . ," I began, but I wasn't sure how to finish the sentence.

"My dad's what?" Ryan asked. "His *funeral*? What about it? You and Jake showed up, but I never heard from you guys again. You know what that means? You didn't come to support me; you came to make yourselves look better. As though you actually cared. Or maybe you just came to schmooze with the cyclists that showed up? I saw you guys talking with them. Not that I care anymore. I have a new focus—myself. I'm going to become the best cyclist the world has ever seen. If there is anyone standing between me and a first-place finish, I will stomp them. I'm not out to make friends. It's not like I can make them, anyway."

So that was it, I thought. "Geez, Ryan, I'm sorry. We didn't mean for it to seem that way."

"Whatever." He turned and stormed through the door that led into the training facility as Dr. V exited the bathroom.

"Ryan has anger issues," Dr. V said in a low voice as he walked over to me. "It is understandable. Losing a parent is devastating. Once you start riding as teammates, he'll warm back up to you."

I wasn't so sure about that.

Hú Dié returned, pulling one of her suitcases, while Murphy pulled the other and held a loop of wire. They both were sweating like Arizona marathon runners in August.

"What have you got in these here bags?" Murphy asked her. "Seem a little on the heavy side."

"I'll show you," she replied. She laid her bag on the polished concrete floor, opened a small combination lock, and then zipped back the large front panel. The top half of the suitcase was clothes that had been stuffed into large ziplock bags, presumably to keep them clean. The bottom half was tools, as I'd suspected.

Hú Dié removed her white gloves and pulled her hair back into a ponytail, tying it off with a zip tie from her suitcase. She grabbed a pair of tin snips and said, "Give me five minutes. Phoenix, why don't you go put on the padded shorts I made for you?"

Dr. V looked at me and raised an eyebrow. I turned away, embarrassed.

"You can change in the shop bathroom," Dr. V said. "I'll give you a proper tour of the facility after your ride."

I sulked out to the SUV and found it unlocked. I grabbed my padded cargo shorts from my backpack and headed into the small bathroom. I didn't really need the shorts for just one lap, but I wanted to get out of sight for a few minutes. It would be good to let Hú Dié be the center of attention. This was her chance to show off, and I knew she needed to impress Dr. V if she was going to be allowed to stick around and hopefully help me out.

I waited several minutes before stepping back out into the shop. Most of the previously air-conditioned space had been overwhelmed by the heat pouring in through the open bay door. Everyone inside was now sweating as much as I was. Hú Dié had already finished the pedal cages and was adjusting the angle of the bike's drop-style handlebars as Dr. V held on to the frame.

"She has already lowered the seat, too," Dr. V said to me as I approached. "Now she's tweaking the bars. She is incredibly fast, and I've never seen anyone do this without a tape measure. I can't wait to see how it fits."

"You will see right now," Hú Dié said, stepping back from the bike. "Try it, Phoenix."

Dr. V handed the bike to me, and I threw a leg over it, straddling the top tube.

"Looks like a great fit," Dr. V said. "Take it for a spin."

"Wait a minute," Hú Dié said. She walked over to the shelf full of helmets, picked one, tore it out of its box, and adjusted the strap length before tossing the helmet to me.

I strapped it on. Of course it fit perfectly.

"Amazing," Dr. V said.

Hú Dié smiled.

I slipped my right foot into Hú Dié's makeshift pedal cage and rode out the bay door, then slipped my left foot into its cage. The cages worked flawlessly.

As critical as I was about cyclocross bikes and the sport itself, I'd never been on a 'cross bike before. The bizarre combination of road bike frame and mountain bike–type tires wasn't nearly as bad as I'd imagined. In fact, I kind of liked it.

The bike fit me just right, and I found the different body position refreshing. A person generally sat more upright on a mountain bike, and leaning forward as I was now made me feel more in control. The bike also made me feel fast, mostly because it *was* fast. Between the different-sized drive sprocket and the much larger wheels, this bike traveled much farther with each revolution of my feet compared with a mountain bike. The knobby tires gripped the dirt surprisingly well, and before I knew it, I found myself tearing through the low grass behind the building. The bike didn't even need to be on the compacted dirt course. I had an overwhelming urge to rip across the field toward the hills and see what I could do with this thing.

"Looks like a winner!" Dr. V called out. "Both the bike fit and the rider. You're quite the sprinter, Phoenix.

Get back here and let's see how you do against my nephew."

I returned to the workshop, and Dr. V said something to Murphy. Murphy disappeared into the training facility, returning with two full water bottles. Ryan was with him. Murphy handed one bottle to Ryan and tossed the other to me. Ryan and I both took long drinks, then shoved our matching team bottles into the matching water bottle cages attached to the down tubes of our matching bikes. Except for the way our feet connected to the pedals, our equipment was identical, right down to matching mini tire pumps also bolted to the bikes.

Ryan scowled at me. "Let's do this."

He climbed onto his bike and took off out of the workshop. I rode after him on my bike, followed by Dr. V, Hú Dié, and Murphy. Ryan stopped at the start/finish line, and I pulled up even with him, several feet to one side. There was no point in our getting jammed up on a course this wide.

Dr. V looked at me. "The route is simple enough. Murphy did an excellent job with the course. All you need to do is point your bike forward and ride."

"If you get lost," Ryan said, "you can just follow my tracks."

Hú Dié giggled, and Ryan turned to her. "Pretty funny, aren't I?" he asked.

"Yes, you are," she replied, looking at his legs.

Ryan flexed his quads. "Can't stop staring at my muscles?"

Hú Dié giggled again. "I was laughing about your seat height. It's a full two centimeters too high. You're riding top-heavy."

"Ha!" Dr. V said. "I've been telling him that for two days."

Ryan frowned. "I'm out of here. Somebody count to three so we can start."

"What's wrong?" I asked. "Can't you count that high yourself?"

Ryan began to blush, and he blasted down the course without waiting for the three-count.

I took off after him.

I fumbled with the bike's foreign gearshift mechanism for a second—short levers on the handlebar stem—and then I got the hang of it and shifted smoothly through the chain ring until I'd caught Ryan and passed him. *Nobody* could outsprint me when my legs were fresh.

Hú Dié hollered from somewhere behind me, and I grinned. I liked the fact that people could see me. I kept hammering, weaving my way effortlessly through the course's twists and turns. The bike fishtailed every now and then, but nowhere near as badly as I would have guessed. I liked this sport more and more. The true test, however, was coming up—hills and trees.

I was a full sixty feet in front of Ryan when I reached the trees and barreled over the first hill, out of sight of the others. The bike handled the transition like a dream. The course was smooth and the slopes weren't too steep, and I was actually enjoying myself. I crossed over a narrower trail that ran perpendicular to the course, and I wondered where it led. It looked as if it might be an old horse trail. I would have to ask Murphy about it. I wanted to give this bike a try over more rugged terrain sometime.

I rode on for another few minutes, excited by unusual thorny scrub trees and the occasional cactus, when I heard Ryan grunt. I looked over my shoulder and saw that he was less than twenty feet behind me and coming up fast.

I could hardly believe it. Ryan had done the same thing back in Indiana. The big ape might not be able to sprint, but he sure had stamina and a lot of heart. His entire head was as red as a tomato, and he was gulping air like a dying fish, but he was gaining.

I gave it all I had, but it wasn't enough. I'd burned myself out on my initial sprint. Ryan caught up with me and threw a punch at my ear. I tapped my brake levers and turned my head, barely missing the blow.

Ryan pulled ahead.

I spat and hammered as hard as I possibly could, determined to catch Ryan, but I couldn't.

We rounded a bend and went over a hill, and I saw that we had looped back into the field. I heard a cowbell begin to ring, and I could just make out Hú Dié jumping up and down in the distance, swinging the bell like a madwoman. She must have had it stuffed in one of her suitcases.

Cowbells were synonymous with cyclocross racing for some reason. Fans rang them endlessly during events. I had always thought that like the sport itself, ringing cow-bells was silly. Now that I heard one while I was racing,

I found it music to my ears. I felt a burst of energy coming on, and I began to hammer.

I managed to close much of the gap between me and Ryan, but he still reached the sand pit twenty feet ahead of me. I watched his wheels sink surprisingly deep as he trudged through the sand, and I started to worry. I'd ridden in sand before, but my wide mountain bike tires never sank as much as Ryan's thinner cyclocross tires were doing. I switched to my rear wheel's tiny "granny gear" and crossed my fingers.

I plowed into the sand, and my feet went from 120 revolutions per minute to fewer than 60. I didn't sink as far as Ryan, because I weighed much less, but I still struggled. I remembered reading that cyclocross races were often held at golf courses, where the route's three different terrains consisted of grass, pavement, and multiple sand traps. I didn't know how those participants did it. Riding in sand was the worst.

Even so, by the time I made it out of the pit, I'd closed the gap with Ryan by another five feet. Next up was the mud bog.

I recalled how Ryan caught me in the muck meadow back in Indiana, and I knew better than to take it slow and easy here. I continued to crank like a precision machine running on high-octane fuel as we neared the final terrain change.

Ryan splashed into the bog first, and I saw him teeter atop his too-high seat. I was sure that he was going to go down, but he managed to rise up out of the saddle and regain his balance. I frowned.

I hit the mud with all the grace of a pig wallowing in its sty. Sticky goop flew up from both tires, splattering me from head to toe. Without goggles, the mud plastered my face, going up my nose and collecting on my eyelashes. I struggled to keep my mouth closed while still trying to breathe. This was ridiculous. I worked my lungs and legs to death as I motored through the bog but found I hadn't gained an inch on Ryan by the time I reached dry land again.

I wiped a muddy arm across my muddy face and saw the three plank hurdles coming up next. I had a decision to make. While most riders got off their bikes to clear the hurdles, there was another way to go about it. I'd heard that some riders bunny-hopped over them. I was very good at bunny hopping with my mountain bike, but I rarely did it at high speed.

Ryan was still riding out of his saddle, and I watched as he unclipped his right foot. He swung his leg behind his seat and over the rear tire to the opposite side of the bike; then he unclipped his left foot and hopped to the ground at a dead run. As he seamlessly shouldered his bike and jumped over the first hurdle, I made up my mind. There was no way I could do that with pedal cages.

When my front tire was two feet away from the first hurdle, I yanked my handlebars up and back as though pulling a wheelie. To my surprise, my oversized front wheel cleared the hurdle. I positioned my feet parallel to the ground and sprang into the air, working my knees as if I were shooting a basketball. Then I lifted my caged feet high and leaned forward, and the bike hopped over the hurdle in a smooth arc like the cow jumping over the moon. I pulled up on the handlebars one last time as I landed, and both tires hit the ground simultaneously in a perfect ending to the bunny hop.

I heard Hú Dié scream with delight, and Dr. V whooped his approval. I completed the task two more times, nearly crashing on my third attempt because my arms and shoulders were so fatigued. Cyclocross was hard work.

I looked over to see Ryan clipping into his pedals after having cleared the last hurdle. He'd jumped back onto his bike without ever breaking stride. He was very good with transitions, but my bunny hopping was better. I was now less than three feet behind him.

The gap between us remained the same until we reached the final obstacle—the Wooden Tightrope. Ryan breezed out of his pedals and hit the ground running again, while I had to fuss with my cages. Ryan hurried up the stairs two at a time with his bike over his shoulder, and he began to race across the elevated plank. By the time I got off my bike, shouldered my ride, and reached the top of the staircase, Ryan was already more than half-way across the plank's thirty-foot length. I was going to lose. Even if Ryan and I were neck and neck running down the other staircase, Ryan would still win because of his superior ability to jump back onto his bike.

I *hate* to lose.

Fifteen feet in the air, I climbed back onto my bike. "Phoenix, no!" Hú Dié shouted.

"Don't do it, Phoenix!" Dr. V called out. "You've already impressed me!"

I ignored them. This obstacle wasn't meant to be ridden, but I didn't care. I'd ridden across planks before on my mountain bike, as well as down countless stairs. However, my mountain bike had a shock-absorbing front fork, smaller wheels, and very different frame and handlebar geometries. I had no idea how this was going to go.

As soon as Ryan reached the far staircase and began to run down it, I started pedaling. I reached the end of the platform and felt gravity suck my front wheel down the stairs. I rose out of my seat and sank behind it as if I were riding down a steep slope on a mountain bike. Below me, I saw Ryan leap off the final stair tread and hit the dirt running.

An instant later, the ground came up to meet me. I pulled up hard on my front wheel so that both tires hit the ground simultaneously like the end of a bunny hop. The impact of the rigid bike on the compacted dirt jarred me as if I'd been dropped off a single-story building, but I held my line and the bike steered true, and I zipped past Ryan as he was jumping back onto his bike. He lunged toward me in an illegal last-ditch effort to grab my jersey, but I swerved out of the way.

I sprinted across the start/finish line two bike lengths ahead of Ryan. Hú Dié howled like a banshee and ran over to me as I eased to a stop. She gave me a huge hug and rang her cowbell in my ear.

Ryan breezed past, shaking his sweaty, helmeted

head. Several beads of sweat flew off his face and landed on my cheek. I whisked them away, but felt the hairs stand on the back of my neck. It took a moment for me to figure out why.

I smelled something familiar—dragon bone.

Ryan raced off toward the hills, alone, and Dr. V came over to me and shook my hand. "That was the gutsiest series of moves I've ever seen! And the sprint you did at the beginning was spectacular! How long have you been riding cyclocross?"

I was sucking more wind than a four-hundred-pound tuba player at the end of a ten-mile march, and I was furious about having smelled dragon bone in Ryan's sweat, but I managed to keep my cool and say, "That was my first time on a 'cross bike."

Dr. V looked me in the eye. "You're telling the truth, aren't you?"

I nodded.

"Phoenix, my boy, you might just be the find of the century."

I shrugged and grabbed my water bottle. I wiped a clump of mud from the nozzle and drank half the contents in three swallows; then I took off my helmet and flung a pint of sweat from my brow. It was *hot* in Texas.

"You look a little warm," Dr. V said. "Let's all go inside and cool off. I can give you the tour now; then you can take a shower. I could use one, too."

Dr. V headed for the workshop, and I rubbed my cheek hard with my hand.

"What are you doing?" Hú Dié asked.

"Ryan is taking dragon bone," I whispered. "The stuff makes your sweat stink. Some of his sweat got on me. I can still smell it."

"Are you sure?"

"Positive. Dr. V is definitely behind this. I can't believe Ryan is taking the stuff. Keep an eye out during the tour. Maybe we'll learn something. Go catch up with Dr. V before he gets suspicious about us whispering."

Hú Dié nodded and hurried toward Dr. V. He waited for her at the workshop's inner door, and she followed him through it.

I pushed my bike into the workshop and leaned it against one of the shelves. I saw Murphy sitting on top of the long workbench. He nodded and threw me a clean shop rag.

I nodded back, and wiped the mud from my face, arms, and legs. "Nice job on the course," I said. "I like it. A lot."

"Thank you kindly," Murphy replied. "Don't know much about bicycles, but what I saw you do out there was impressive. Hats off to you." He lifted his straw cowboy hat a few inches off his head to salute me, and his

T-shirt rode up on his hip. I saw a large revolver in a holster attached to his belt.

My eyes widened.

Murphy grinned. "Welcome to Texas, son."

I dropped the rag and got the heck out of there. Murphy was beginning to freak me out.

I slipped off my muddy hiking boots and passed through the door that Hú Dié and Dr. V had just gone through. I found myself in a long, cool, brightly lit corridor. Dr. V and Hú Dié stood at the far end, looking up at one corner where the walls met the ceiling. I followed their gaze and saw a security camera with wires dangling from it.

As I headed down the corridor, Dr. V said to me, "I was just telling your cousin that I take security very seriously. That roll-up bay door for the workshop is normally bolted closed with industrial-grade locks, and the regular doors are only accessible via electronic keycards. I have these security cameras positioned throughout the building. Everything is operational at this time except the cameras, but Murphy should have them hooked up before the team arrives."

I tried to ignore the sinking feeling forming in my gut. It was as if Dr. V knew we intended to snoop around or might try to make a run for it. "When do we get our keycards?" I asked.

"In a few days. In the meantime, just come see me whenever you wish to leave the facility. If I'm not here, see Murphy. He's usually inside working on one thing or another."

"So we're locked in? That seems a little extreme. What if there is a fire?"

"The doors can be opened from the inside without a card. That is a fire ordinance. However, a piercing alarm will sound and the fire department will be alerted. It is better if you simply find one of us if you wish to step outside."

"What if it's the middle of the night?"

"Why would you want to leave in the middle of the night?"

I shrugged. I didn't have a good answer.

"What about me?" Hú Dié asked.

"Yes," Dr. V replied. "What about you? I can't imagine that a young woman with your skills brought along all those tools for a vacation in Los Angeles."

Hú Dié stiffened. "No."

"You wanted to impress me so that I would hire you, didn't you?"

Hú Dié looked him square in the face. "Yes."

Dr. V smiled. "Well, you more than impressed me, and I appreciate a person with drive. I don't know what I can offer you long-term, but short-term I would be grateful if you could stay here at the training facility until my mechanic arrives on Thursday. I'm scheduled to receive a shipment of bike frames this afternoon, and I had planned to spend several days assembling them myself before the team members arrive. However, I'm currently in the middle of another project and would rather not have to deal with the bikes. Perhaps you will assemble them."

"I'd love to!" Hú Dié said.

"Very glad to hear it," Dr. V said. "We will think up some sort of compensation, as I don't recall you having a work visa, only a ninety-day travel visa." He turned to me. "I'm assuming you have no problem with this, as you had to know what she was up to?"

"Actually," I lied, "I didn't know what she was up to, although I suspected something when I saw the extra fees charged for her luggage."

"No worries," Dr. V said. "She appears to be worth it." He smiled at Hú Dié. "I will have the travel agent cancel your stays in L.A. and Austin."

"Um," Hú Dié said, "I was kind of looking forward to going to Austin, if only for half a day."

"Might there be a certain famous bike shop that you wish to visit?"

Hú Dié nodded.

"Not a problem. If you're not too tired, how would you like to head over there an hour from now? Murphy needs to run into the city to get a few things. I could have him drop you off, then pick you up a couple hours later. I'm sure they're open late tonight, as it's Saturday. You can start on the bikes tomorrow."

Hú Dié squealed. "Thank you! I have plenty of energy. I napped on the plane rides. I'll start on the bikes as soon as I get back this evening. I'm anxious to see those, too."

Dr. V nodded. "Sounds good to me. Let's continue the tour."

Dr. V used a doorstop to prop open a door at the end

of the corridor, and Hú Dié and I followed him into a large training space with multiple windows and a door leading outside. Several stationary "trainers" were positioned in a semicircle, facing a large projection screen. The trainers were devices a little larger than milk crates and made from metal tubing. A team member could lock his bike's rear tire into one of these, and the bike instantly became a stationary trainer. Resistance against the tire could be adjusted to simulate different riding conditions, and the rider could even adjust his gears while using the contraption. Best of all, it was the same bike the guy would race on, so he had more practice time with it, even in bad weather.

As for the screen, Dr. V explained that it was part of a high-end training system that connected each of the stationary trainers to a computer that controlled a video projector. Actual race footage from famous courses was projected onto the screen, and the people in the training room could ride along virtually while the computer automatically adjusted the resistance against their rear tires to match the hills and descents in the video.

"I've only seen these in magazines," Hú Dié said. "Can I try it sometime?"

"Of course," Dr. V replied. "Hooking it up is number two on Murphy's to-do list, right after hooking up the security cameras. Come, let me show you the dining area and kitchen."

We walked through a set of swinging double doors into a moderately sized space that contained several sets of tables and chairs. Along one wall were several refrigerators, and along another was a pair of stoves with a long counter next to them. Several microwaves sat on the counter, along with a row of blenders, and there was a huge double sink. A series of shelves hung over the counter, and the shelves were stocked with protein powders, vitamins, electrolytes, energy bars, meal replacement bars, energy gels . . . an endless selection of nutritional supplements. While I ate an energy bar every once in a while, I didn't use the other stuff. Grandfather would have had a fit. He believed I got all the nutrients I needed from a balanced diet and the occasional dose of Chinese herbs. However, I imagined elite athletes might benefit from some of those items.

"Better performance through better chemistry," Dr. V said.

I couldn't help muttering, "Yeah, I've seen Ryan's transformation since last year."

"What are you implying?" Dr. V asked.

I bit my tongue. "Nothing."

"Ryan underwent a growth spurt," Dr. V said. "Pure and simple. Sure, he takes a mountain of vitamins, but that is his choice. He also spent far too much time in my weight room back in Belgium. I keep telling him that he is too big to ride competitively, but he won't listen to me. Just like his seat height. I wish he had fallen flat on his oversized butt back in that mud bog."

Hú Dié giggled.

Dr. V continued. "Since we're discussing supplements,

I made a difficult decision yesterday that you two should know about. Remember I told you about Lin Tan, Phoenix?"

I swallowed hard. "Yes."

"Like everyone who races for Team Vanderhausen, Lin Tan signed an agreement that he wouldn't put anything illegal into his body. He broke that agreement. I had planned to cut him some slack and keep him close to the team throughout his recent suspension, but I changed my mind. I decided that I needed to set an example. I kicked him off the team permanently."

Hú Dié took a deep breath.

Dr. V looked at her. "Do you know Lin Tan?"

"I know of him," she replied, "but I've never met him. I was excited to hear that he was racing for you. Many people in China were. There aren't too many professional Chinese cyclists. Your news makes me sad."

"It saddens me, too," Dr. V said, "but people need to honor their agreements. I will ask you to sign the same document, Phoenix."

"Okay," I said.

"In for a penny, in for a pound," Dr. V said. "As for a way *out*—" He pointed to a door that was equipped with a push bar like the kind you would find on a fire exit. A keycard reader was mounted on the wall next to the door. "This is the door on the front of the building. Again, I should have a keycard for you in a few days. In the meantime, if there is ever a fire or other need to evacuate, head this way, if you can. You can also exit in the training area. Understand?"

"Yes," Hú Dié and I replied in unison.

Dr. V nodded and waved his arm. "Come on, one more area to show you."

We walked through a second set of swinging double doors and entered a long corridor with multiple doors along either wall and a single door at the very end.

"The living quarters," Dr. V said.

He opened the first door to our right, and I saw a small space that reminded me of a hotel room. It contained a bed, a dresser, a nightstand with an alarm clock, a floor lamp, and a flat-screen television hanging on one wall. There was also a window and another door.

Dr. V pointed to the door. "There is a private bathroom in there. It's not much, but it's better than the barracks-style sleeping quarters and community bathrooms many teams have. And every rider gets his own room. Team members are allowed to stay here, or they may rent their own houses outside the ranch, which is what I do. My house is fifteen miles away, near Austin. I may build a home here at the ranch at some point, but for now I believe I will enjoy being able to take a break from team life every night. This is where you will sleep, Phoenix."

"What about Ryan?" I asked.

Dr. V closed the door and then opened the door to our left. The room beyond was a mirror image of my room, except instead of a dresser, there was a desk topped with a computer. There were piles of cycling clothes everywhere.

"Please excuse the mess," Dr. V said, pointing to the

desk. "Ryan wanted *that* instead of a dresser. He also demanded his own high-speed Internet connection because the facility's Wi-Fi wasn't fast enough for him. He is such an Internet junkie."

Dr. V closed the door and turned to Hú Dié. "Pick a room."

Hú Dié walked all the way down the corridor and grabbed the knob of the door at the very end. She tried turning the handle, but it didn't budge.

"Locked," Dr. V said. "That is my private office. No one goes in there except me."

"Sorry," Hú Dié said.

"No problem. Pick any other room."

I walked over to her as she tried another door. It opened into a carbon-copy room of mine.

"I'll take this one," she said. "It's farthest from the boys."

"Perfect," Dr. V said. "I will get you a key so you can lock up your room. I'll get the one for your door, too, Phoenix."

"Thanks," I said.

"Any questions?" Dr. V asked.

"Not right now," I replied.

"Me neither," Hú Dié said.

"Sounds like it's time for a late lunch, then," Dr. V said. "Get your things and put them in your rooms. Meet me in the dining area in ten minutes. I need to let Murphy know about Hú Dié joining him; then I'll whip us up some sandwiches. What do you plan to do while your cousin heads to Austin, Phoenix? Would you like to go as well?"

I shook my head. "No, thanks. I think I'll pass on the field trip. I'm really tired. Maybe I'll take a nap."

"I suggest you only take a short one, then. Otherwise, you'll be up all night. As for me, I plan to head home after the bikes arrive. I usually go to bed early and wake at five a.m."

"What about Ryan?" Hú Dié asked.

"Ryan will be staying here, as he has been," Dr. V said. "I'll make sure he's returned and settled down before I leave, so don't worry. If you should have trouble with him or anything else, let Murphy know. If he's not in the facility working, he'll be in his camper or somewhere on the grounds nearby. There is a telephone in the kitchen. I'll leave his cell phone number next to it. Get your things. I'm hungry." He pushed through the double doors and went to find Murphy.

I looked at Hú Dié. "What do you think?" I whispered.

"I think you're crazy for not going to the bike shop," she replied.

I shook my head and pointed to the locked office door. "I'm talking about *that*."

"No problem. I can get us in *there* anytime. It won't do us any good, though. We can't get out of this building without the door alarm going off and alerting Murphy."

"Wait—how?"

"Ever heard of a bump key?"

"No."

"It's sort of like a master key. Once Dr. V gives me the key to my room, I can modify it to open any lock that is the same model made by the same manufacturer, as long as the lock isn't bump-proof. The locks on these doors aren't bump-proof and they're all the same model. I checked."

I was going to ask Hú Dié how she knew about these things, but then I thought better of it.

"How long will it take you to make it?" I asked.

"About twenty minutes," she replied. "I could do it tonight, if you want, after I have the key to my room."

"Heck, yeah. Let's do it."

"What do you plan to do if we find the dragon bone in there?"

"Grab it and get out of here. Duh."

"Get out how?"

"Bicycles," I said. "I'll ride the bike I just raced, and you can ride Ryan's. His frame is a little big for you, but you can manage."

"What about Murphy?"

"He'll be asleep."

"But he'll wake up when we open the door and the alarm goes off. Haven't you been listening?"

"Can you disarm it?"

"I don't think so. . . ."

"Then we'll ride really fast. I've seen you on a bike. You can hammer."

"I'm not sure this is such a good idea."

I thought for a moment. "What about the bay door

in the workshop? That one might not have an alarm. Can you open its locks?"

"No. I already checked. You told me to keep an eye out, remember?"

"What about that motorcycle outside? That would make for a fast getaway after the exit door alarm sounds. Can you ride it?"

"Probably, but we don't have the starter key, and it's not like I can hot-wire it. Even if we found a key stashed in Dr. V's office, firing it up and figuring out how the gears are configured will take time. I've never ridden one like that. There is also the gate to consider. Bicycles would be better than the motorcycle because we could climb the gate and pull them over with us. However, Murphy could still catch up to us on the road if he came after us. I don't know about this."

"We'll go cross-country, then. Even if Murphy wakes up, he'll never catch us."

"In the dark? There are rattlesnakes and scorpions and coyotes out there. Murphy also has a horse. Take a nap, Phoenix. You're not thinking clearly."

"Are you with me or not?" I asked. "In for a penny, in for a pound."

Hú Dié glared at me as if testing my resolve.

I glared back, my green eyes unyielding.

But then common sense got the better of me. Hú Dié was right. We needed a solid escape plan. "How about if we just sneak into his office and poke around? If we find the dragon bone and a good plan comes to mind, we'll leave. If not, we'll wait."

She sighed. "Fine. Count me in."

"Good," I said. "What time should we do it?"

"I don't know. How about two a.m.?"

"All right. We should get going."

Hú Dié grabbed her things from the shop, and I banged the mud off my hiking boots and put them back on before getting my stuff from the SUV. I unpacked, washed up, and then went to the dining area, where I ate a couple of ham-and-cheese sandwiches with Dr. V, Hú Dié, and Murphy. Ryan didn't join us. He was still off in the hills somewhere.

The bike frames arrived as we were finishing our meal, and Hú Dié oohed and aahed over them until Murphy told her they had to leave. Dr. V said he was going to take one of the SUVs off-road into the hills to find Ryan because he, too, wanted to leave. He gave Hú Dié and me our room keys, and I went and took a long, cool shower.

I was toweling off when Dr. V knocked on my door and said he had found Ryan sulking in his room. Dr. V said he was leaving and would return in the morning.

I waited a couple of minutes, then peered between the slats of my window's mini blinds. I soon saw Dr. V get into one of the black SUVs and head up the dusty road toward the gate.

I set the alarm clock to 1:50 a.m. and climbed into bed, falling asleep the moment my head hit the pillow. I never heard Hú Dié and Murphy return.

I woke to a dark room with an unfamiliar alarm blaring. I sat up and remembered where I was—the Team Vander-hausen training facility. I began to panic, thinking the door alarm was sounding and that Hú Dié was making off with the dragon bone without me, but then I saw a clock that read 1:50 a.m., and I came to my senses. It was just the alarm clock sounding.

I fumbled around in the dark until I managed to turn off the alarm. I didn't turn on the light. I found one of the windows and raised the blinds. Flood lamps illumi-nated the building's perimeter and the carport well enough to see that Dr. V was still gone, and Murphy's camper was dark. The coast was clear.

I closed the blinds and flipped on the light, then quickly dressed and grabbed my key. As an afterthought, I shoved my wallet and passport into one of my cargo pockets. I crept across the corridor to Ryan's room and placed my ear against the door. I could hear him snoring like a freight train. It sounded as if he was in the middle of a deep dragon bone sleep. Grandfather often snored like that. So far, so good.

I walked down the corridor and knocked softly on Hú Dié's door, but no one answered.

I knocked harder. Still no answer.

I headed for the workshop. I passed through the dining area, the training area, and the other long corridor, entering the workshop to find Hú Dié hunched over the workbench, filing a key that was clamped in a vice.

"Hi," I said.

Hú Dié nearly jumped through the roof.

"Don't scare me like that!" she barked. She was a haggard mess. She had dark, puffy circles beneath her eyes, and her eyelids drooped with fatigue. She'd changed out of her sundress and sandals and was now wearing cargo shorts and a T-shirt that read MELLOW JOHNNY'S. That was the name of Lance Armstrong's bike shop.

"Are you all right?" I asked.

"Yeah. Just tired. The jet lag has caught up with me."

I looked around the workshop and saw that bike components had been arranged into neat piles on the floor, one set of components for each new frame. There were hundreds of parts in each pile, from nuts to bolts to cables. Sorting all of that out had to have taken hours.

"You haven't slept at all?" I asked.

"Not since the airplanes."

"Were you too excited from your trip to the bike shop? Or are you worried about what we're gonna do?"

"Both, I guess. There's no way I could sleep, knowing what is about to happen. Sorting all this stuff helped to occupy my mind and my time."

"You still want to do it?"

"In for a penny, in for a pound," she said. "Let's get it over with. The key is finished." She unclamped the key and held it up to a work light. I saw that all the peaks of the key's teeth had been filed to a uniform height. Hú Dié grabbed a rubber mallet and headed for the door I had just come through.

"What's the mallet for?" I asked.

"It's a bump key, remember?" she said. "I need something to bump it with."

As we left the workshop, I told her about Ryan's snoring and reminded her that dragon bone makes people sleep deeply.

"Let's hope he stays that way," she said.

"He will," I said. "I still can't believe he's taking it."

Hú Dié said nothing.

"So, how was your trip to the bike shop?" I asked.

The question seemed to perk her up. "It was great," she said. "I was expecting more of a souvenir shop than an actual bike shop, but I was wrong. They have all kinds of bikes for sale, plus a great service area right in the middle of everything. The bike mechanics are like rock stars."

"Rock stars?"

"Yes. Everyone can see everything the mechanics are doing. The service area has glass display cabinets around it with stools on the outside, and they have a great coffee and smoothie bar next to the service area. People can grab something to drink, then sit down and watch the mechanics in action."

"Cool. Is there anything else?"

"In the basement they have an indoor training area, plus a bunch of bikes on display that Armstrong rode in different races over the years. It's like a museum of technological cycling advancements."

"Maybe I should check it out."

"You should. They sell gear for many different types of riding, including mountain biking. In fact, I bought you something." We reached her room, and she opened the unlocked door. She unplugged a long black object from an outlet near the doorway and handed it to me.

I turned it over in my hands. It was a small, rechargeable headlamp that could be mounted to a helmet with a strap. "You bought this for me?" I asked. "For our escape?"

She nodded. "We can use it while we're poking around, too."

"Thank you! Where's yours?"

Hú Dié looked away. "I could only afford to buy one."

"Oh," I said, embarrassed. I held the headlamp out to her. "Why don't you keep it, then?"

Her face darkened. "It's a gift. For you. From me."

I felt myself begin to blush. "I'm sorry. I am such an idiot. Thank you very much."

"You're welcome," she replied, still not looking at me. "Can we please do this?"

I slipped the charger into one of my oversized pockets and palmed the headlamp. "Okay."

Hú Dié reached down and picked up a threadbare hydration backpack from the floor. She must have brought it in one of her suitcases. "This pack isn't in as good condition as the one we left at Cangzhen Temple," she said, "but it's better than nothing. I took the bladder out to make room for the dragon bone, in case we find it and decide to escape tonight."

"Good thinking."

She closed the door to her room, and we walked to Dr. V's office door. Hú Dié slipped the bump key partway into the doorknob lock and gripped the doorknob with one hand while pinching the key between her thumb and index finger of the same hand. She twisted the knob and key slightly, then tapped the key with the mallet that she held in her other hand.

I caught my breath as I heard metal pins within the lock jingle, and the key slipped a few millimeters deeper into the lock. I watched as Hú Dié kept the tension on the doorknob and key and tapped again. The pins within the lock jingled a second time, and the key slipped even farther into the lock. She repeated the process one more time, and the key went all the way in. Hú Dié turned the key and the knob simultaneously, and the door opened.

"Unbelievable," I said. "That was the coolest thing I've ever seen!"

"You need to hang out in Kaifeng more," Hú Dié replied. She stepped away from the door. "After you."

I flipped on the headlamp and walked through the doorway. My breath caught in my throat again. This was not at all what I was expecting.

Hú Dié walked in behind me. "Oh, my goodness," she said.

We were standing in a laboratory. I flashed the bright light around the room. It was about thirty feet square and filled with machines. Tiny lights blinked and computer panels glowed. There was enough light from the instrument panels that we probably didn't even need the flashlight. Some of the freestanding equipment, like IV drips and oxygen tanks, I recognized from my visits to the nursing home. Other things, however, looked like gadgets from a spaceship flight deck.

A steel counter ran along two of the walls, containing a wide array of microscopes, petri dishes, and other items. Above one counter was a pair of windows covered with blinds. On the floor in one corner was what appeared to be a small kiln. Next to the kiln was a shelved cabinet containing fossilized bones.

"Look," I said, pointing to the bones. "It looks like Dr. V is trying to make his own dragon bone."

"That doesn't surprise me," Hú Dié said. "Check this out. I think I found his office."

I turned to her in the eerie machine glow. She was staring at one of the walls, which contained a bank of mirrored windows and a door.

I headed for the office door, skirting a tall row of machines set in the center of the room, when I noticed a strange light atop one of the devices. I looked up and saw three skylights ten feet overhead. Mechanical blinds prevented any light from entering the room through two of the skylights, but the blinds over the third were partially open. Moonlight trickled in. I could even make out a few stars.

I pointed up. "We'll have a clear night if we decide to make a break for it."

Hú Dié didn't reply.

I glanced over and saw that she was now standing beside a stainless-steel table, next to one of the banks of machines. I turned my flashlight in that direction and headed toward her, and my jaw dropped.

There was a clipboard on the table like the one my uncle used at the nursing home. On the clipboard was a medical chart. Across the top of the chart was a name: *Ryan Vanderhausen.*

"No way!" I said, grabbing the chart and looking it over. "Dr. V is running experiments on his own nephew! And look . . . Ryan is taking *way* too much dragon bone compared with what my grandfather uses. It looks like he's been using it for . . . six months? How can this be?"

"I have no idea," Hú Dié said. "Let's just do what we came here to do." She went to one of the counters.

I shook my head and walked over to Dr. V's office door. There was a keypad next to it. I tried the door, but it was locked. I was about to ask Hú Dié to come over and determine whether she could break in here, too, when a small light turned on across the room. Hú Dié called out, "Found it!"

I looked over and saw that she had switched on a short fluorescent fixture mounted to the bottom of a wall cabinet. Beneath the cabinet was a counter with two dragon-shaped vessels. One was Grandfather's. The other had to be PawPaw's.

"Good work!" I said.

Hú Dié nodded. She reached into her pack and removed a large fabric bag.

"What's that?" I asked.

"A silk drawstring bag," she replied in an odd tone.

"What are you doing?"

"Those containers won't fit in my pack. I need to carry the dragon bone somehow."

"You want to take the dragon bone and escape right now?"

"Yes." She opened the bag.

I began to walk toward her, when I noticed lights flickering behind the window blinds. I ran to one of the windows and poked my fingers between the blinds' slats. I peered out to see an unfamiliar dusty pickup truck pull up less than twenty feet from the building.

"Someone is coming!" I said.

Hú Dié didn't reply.

I stared at the truck. There was a long extension ladder in the truck bed, and the front of the vehicle was dented and scraped, with several strands of barbed wire clinging to the grill. The truck had gotten onto the property by busting through a fence. The driver and passenger got out, and my heart nearly stopped. "It's Lin Tan and Meathead!" I gasped.

I looked back at Hú Dié. She stiffened, but still said nothing.

She didn't even look surprised.

I felt the blood drain from my face. Was Hú Dié double-crossing me? Had she worked out a secret deal with her crush, Lin Tan? She began to dump the dragon bone into the silk bag, and I realized that the bag looked just like the one Lin Tan had used back at Cangzhen Temple when he stole Grandmaster Long's dragon bone.

I heard shouting outside and couldn't resist turning back to the window.

It was Murphy. He had his gun drawn and was walking toward the rented truck. Lin Tan had a gun, too. The Texan and the Chinese cyclist pointed their weapons at one another, but Meathead sprang into action first. One of his hands was wrapped in heavy bandages, and I remembered that Hú Dié had smashed his hand with her elbow back at Cangzhen Temple. The injury didn't seem to matter. He grabbed a section of the ladder from the back of the truck, and while Murphy watched Lin Tan,

Meathead thrust the ladder at Murphy. Murphy fired as the lowest rung struck his gun hand.

The bullet buried itself harmlessly in the side of the truck, and Meathead twisted the ladder. The ladder's feet spun around, knocking the gun from Murphy's hand. Murphy lunged to pick up his gun, but Lin Tan jumped on him and pistol-whipped him in the back of the head. Murphy's body collapsed like a deflated balloon.

I turned to Hú Dié. The silk bag was now tied shut, and she was pouring the last of the dragon bone from one of the dragon vessels into a large glass test tube that she must have grabbed from the counter.

"What are you doing?" I shouted.

Hú Dié remained silent. She pushed a rubber stopper into the test tube.

I took a step toward her.

"Please," she said finally. "Don't make this any more difficult than it already is. Stay right where you are."

I laughed. I couldn't help myself. "You really *are* psycho. You think I'm going to just let you walk out of here with my dragon bone?"

"*Your* dragon bone? What gives you any more right to it than me, now that someone else has stolen it?"

I couldn't believe my ears. Then again, Hú Dié and her father earned their living as forgers of documents and bicycles. Their sense of responsibility was skewed. Why should I expect not to get tricked, too? I should have paid more attention to PawPaw's warning.

"How long have you been planning to hang me out to dry?" I asked.

Hú Dié took a step toward me. "I'm not hanging you out to dry. Lin Tan doesn't even know you're here. Take this—" She held out the test tube. "Hide somewhere until I've left with those two goons. Use the headlamp I gave you. Escape to your grandfather."

"I'm not going anywhere without *all* of the dragon bone."

"Lin Tan and the other guy are not killers, but they may make an exception if they find you here. Leave now. Please."

"I really am an idiot. I actually thought you were my friend."

"I am your friend. It's just that I have priorities. I need to help my mother."

"Your mother? You said that she no longer lives with you."

"She doesn't. She lives in a nursing home, even though she is not that old. She has what you Westerners call ALS, or Lou Gehrig's disease. Her nerve cells are wasting away, and she has lost her ability to walk or even move her arms and head normally. I want to see if dragon bone can help."

"But . . . you can't give her dragon bone."

"Why not? Because she isn't part of your grandfather's little club?"

I ground my teeth. "Why didn't you say something about her earlier?"

"Because it's none of your business. It still isn't, in fact. I don't know why I'm wasting my time telling you now."

Anger began to swell within me. "You never answered my question. How long have you been planning this?"

"A few hours."

"What?"

"All of this just came together. That's why I didn't get any sleep. It's too fresh in my mind, and the more I think about it, the worse I feel. Lin Tan and the other guy—his name is Bjorn—were downtown renting that pickup truck when they saw Murphy with me in the passenger seat. They recognized me from Cangzhen Temple and followed us to the bike store. After Murphy left, Lin Tan approached me inside the bike shop. It was the first time I'd ever spoken with him. I swear. He told me everything that he has gone through with Dr. V, from the beginning. He knew more than half a year ago that he might be suspended. However, Dr. V told him that he would cover for him if he did a few special side projects. That's why he got involved."

"What do you mean by 'side projects'? Spying on my grandfather and stealing his dragon bone?"

"Yes. Lin Tan began watching your house in November, and he stole a small amount of dragon bone in December to give to Dr. V. Lin Tan didn't know what the substance was until recently."

I thought about how my uncle had managed to take some of Grandfather's dragon bone without his noticing.

Lin Tan stealing some back then would explain how Ryan had been taking it for so long.

"Lin Tan did all of this for a chance to ride?" I asked.

"Mostly. He and Bjorn were also paid a lot of money, but he was mainly interested in continuing his racing career. This wasn't his first suspension, and he didn't think anyone else would pick him up. Dr. V was his last hope. Once Lin Tan brought the latest batch of dragon bone to Dr. V from China, though, Dr. V paid him and Bjorn, and then Dr. V kicked both of them out of his organization, anyway."

"And how do you fit in?"

"Lin Tan and Bjorn decided to come back here to steal the dragon bone. They plan to sell it and form their own team. They thought that having me on the inside would help them break in, and they promised to let me have some dragon bone for my mother. Their plan was solid, so I agreed. Also, Bjorn set up the security system here. If anyone can get in and out without tripping alarms, it's him. *My* plan was—and still is—to double-cross them and take all the dragon bone for myself. Of course, I planned to give some of it to you so that you can share it with your grandfather, and return some to Grandmaster Long and that woman, PawPaw. Not that I expect you to believe me."

"You're right about that. If you really planned to give me some dragon bone, you would have brought *two* bags." I took another step toward her.

She slipped the tube of dragon bone into one of her

cargo pants' pockets and said, "That's far enough. I don't have another bag. This glass tube is the best I can do, but it sounds like you don't want it. Come one step closer, and I'll break your arms."

I felt my upper lip curl back. "Promise?"

"In for a penny, in for a pound," she said.

"Shut up and ride," I replied.

I never imagined that I could actually hit a girl, but when I saw the look on her face, I knew that I had to make an exception. I took a step toward Hú Dié, and she flipped on the overhead lights. As I blinked against the sudden brightness, she attacked. She swung her right forearm at my head, and I ducked, realizing too late that it was just a ploy to get me to lower my head. Her powerful thigh rose up, and her knee slammed into my jaw.

I dropped the headlamp and reeled back as if I'd been hit with a brick. I saw stars, as well as Hú Dié's forearm coming once more at my face. I slid to one side, dodging the blow, but I tripped and went down flat onto my back. Hú Dié stepped up next to me, swinging one leg back to soccer-kick my head off my shoulders, and I up-kicked her square in the groin.

She doubled over. That cheap shot hurts girls almost as much as it hurts guys.

I was halfway to my feet when Hú Dié attacked again. She dove on top of me, knocking me to the ground. I tried to push her off, but she managed to wrap her legs around my midsection.

Hú Dié began to squeeze. I felt every bit of air rush out of my lungs. I tried to inhale, but it was no use. Her legs were too strong. My diaphragm couldn't expand. In a panic, I began to hammer my fists against her thighs, but she didn't let up. The world started to turn gray around me, and my eyes locked on to hers.

She was crying.

CRASH!

The sky exploded above me.

I blinked and saw Hú Dié lean forward to shield me as a shower of glass rained down over both of us. The tension in her legs lessened, and I managed to twist free. I tried to stand but was too dizzy. I sat down hard on a thousand shards of safety glass and looked up at what remained of one of the skylights.

Bjorn stared back at me. The big guy had a section of the mechanical blinds in one hand and a large crowbar in the other. He dropped the blinds to the floor, narrowly missing Hú Dié, who was scrambling to her feet. Bjorn disappeared, only to reappear an instant later with the extension ladder. He quickly lowered the ladder into the room through the skylight opening. Lin Tan's head appeared in the skylight, next to Bjorn's, and Lin Tan shouted something to Hú Dié in Chinese.

Hú Dié sniffled and looked at me. "Goodbye, Phoenix."

I tried to get to my feet once more, when two gunshots boomed across the room.

BANG! BANG!

Hú Dié screamed, and Bjorn tumbled through the skylight. He landed in a heap on the floor. The second shot struck Lin Tan, and he reeled backward before collapsing onto the roof with a thud.

Hú Dié screamed again, and I looked across the room toward the mirrored wall. The door to Dr. V's office was slightly ajar. The door opened fully, and Dr. V stepped through it. He was holding a scoped rifle.

Dr. V aimed the rifle at me and grinned. "Welcome to Texas, son."

I rubbed my eyes, unsure if I was awake or if Hú Dié had squeezed me unconscious and I was dreaming this whole thing.

I wasn't dreaming.

Hú Dié had double-crossed me, and Dr. V was aiming a rifle at my face. Lin Tan and Bjorn were dead, and Ryan was dead to the world in a dragon bone stupor. I couldn't possibly have dreamed up something this crazy.

Dr. V turned the rifle toward Hú Dié and said, "Nice try, young lady. You and Phoenix, go stand next to that steel table."

I got to my feet and found that my sense of balance had returned. I walked over and stood on the side of the table near Ryan's medical chart. Hú Dié did the smart thing and stood on the opposite side. If I were standing next to her, I might have wrung her neck, and she knew it.

"Surprised to see me?" Dr. V asked.

I opened my mouth to answer but realized that Dr. V was speaking to Hú Dié.

"Yes," Hú Dié replied. "How did you get to the ranch without me noticing your truck? I've been awake all night."

Dr. V smiled. "I rode my bike!" He stepped out into the lab and nodded toward his office doorway. I looked into the office and saw a dirty cyclocross bike resting next to another door along the office's back wall. He must have come in that way. I'd never seen that side of the building and had no idea there was a door.

"How did you know to come tonight?" Hú Dié asked.

"The video cameras," Dr. V said. "Those dangling wires you saw? Decoys. Every camera in this building is fully functional, complete with sound-amplifying microphones. They feed into a security computer in my office and are accessible via the Internet. Murphy was watching you from his trailer, and I was watching you from home. I played back some of the recorded footage from earlier today and learned what you and Phoenix were up to. Once I arrived here, I watched you both from my office computer, and finally through these two-way mirrors. If it makes you feel any better, you didn't stand a chance." He looked at me. "You either."

I glowered at him.

"The funny thing is," Dr. V continued, "I didn't know a thing about Lin Tan's plan until he showed up with Bjorn. I can't say that their actions surprise me, though, and I have to admit, Hú Dié, that bump key you made is impressive. I'll never let Murphy live that one down. He should have thought to put a better lock on my lab door. He also should have put some kind of alarm on these skylights."

"What are you going to do with us?" Hú Dié asked.

Dr. V nodded toward the cabinet of fossils and the kiln. "I've been working to reverse-engineer dragon bone and determine its primary chemical properties. Those are ordinary fossilized animal bones, but I plan to cook them up soon, along with a few additives, and synthesize my own true dragon bone. More guinea pigs would be nice." He grinned.

I swallowed hard. "Why synthesize it? You have enough to last you hundreds of years."

"This has nothing to do with my longevity. I didn't even know about dragon bone's life-extending properties until I read translations of your grandfather's telephone calls with that woman PawPaw. I only suspected that it improved physical performance after seeing how spry your grandfather is. I'll never forget how gracefully he moved at my brother's funeral. No one his age can move like that without extraordinary chemical or biological assistance. Based on what little experimentation I've done thus far, I see that I was correct about dragon bone's effects."

I glanced at the chart on the table. "You said '*more* guinea pigs.' You're testing it on Ryan, aren't you?"

"Very good."

Hú Dié pointed a finger at him. "You're planning to

mass-produce it so you can give it to your race team members!"

Dr. V shook his head. "While that is true, I've recently begun to imagine bigger things. Just think . . . sports drinks with dragon bone, energy bars—I'll make a fortune."

"You already have a fortune," I said.

Dr. V smiled. "Then I'll have two fortunes."

"You're putting people's lives in danger," I said. "Do you have any idea what is happening to Ryan right now? He's still asleep after all this noise, I bet."

"I believe so. When a person takes dragon bone, they slip into a nearly unconscious state. It is extraordinary. I've never seen anything like it."

"The dragon bone is taking control of him," I said. "It is coming to life."

"That's nonsense."

"It's not! Look at my grandfather. Do you know where he is now? A nursing home. If you take it too long and then stop, you will die. It becomes one with you. Ryan needs to stop."

"He is already stopping. He had been consuming a smaller amount each day with his dinner for a while, but he told me yesterday evening that he is done with it. He only tried it because he thought he might finally be able to beat you in a race. After you still beat him, he said he was through with the substance. I don't plan on forcing him to continue taking it. At least, not until I understand it better."

I gave a small sigh of relief. Ryan was being a jerk,

but I didn't want anything bad to happen to him. "It won't be easy for him to quit," I said. "Make him exercise. Sweating will help."

"Interesting," Dr. V said. "I didn't know that. I noticed an aroma around him when he was sweating profusely. Thank you for telling me. Is there anything else I should know?"

"You should know that you can't keep me and Hú Dié here. People will come looking for us. You have to let us go."

Dr. V chuckled. "I'm sure that people will come looking for you. That's why I plan to offer you a deal, Phoenix. Ride for me, and I'll send some dragon bone to your grandfather."

My heart skipped a beat. "Ride for you? For how long?"

"Years, if you do as well as I anticipate."

"What if I say no?"

"Then your grandfather will die."

I shuddered. "If my grandfather dies, then there's no reason for me to continue riding for you."

Dr. V grinned. "That's a chance I'm willing to take. Would you really let your grandfather die simply because you do not want to ride for me?"

I banged my fist against my thigh. "Why me? You should find some adult pro to blackmail. I'm just a kid."

"You are not a kid. You are an extraordinary young man. After what I saw you do on the course yesterday, I'm certain you could already beat many of the professional adult cyclocross racers out there. With proper training, you could very well beat *all* the adult professionals before you even finish high school. Ryan's father and I both raced professionally when we were just teenagers. I know what I'm talking about. Additionally, you have a special look and charm about you. Your ethnicity is ambiguous. You are a marketer's dream. You will be famous! I will make you the poster boy for my dragon bone sports drinks and energy bars."

I glanced at the chart on the table again. "What about Ryan?"

"Ryan is a good cyclist, but he will never be a great cyclist. You are already a great cyclist."

I frowned. "If I agree to ride for you, how much dragon bone will you send to my grandfather?".

"Enough to keep him alive one week at a time. I've watched a month's worth of video recordings of him putting dragon bone into his morning tea, so I believe I have a good sense of how much will suffice. I will continue the weekly shipments as long as you continue to give me your best effort. If I suspect that you are slacking off, or if you attempt to leave without my permission or try to contact authorities or disrupt my organization in any way, I will cut off his supply."

I ground my teeth and looked at my watch. It was 2:30 a.m., Sunday morning. "When would you send the first shipment? Today? Tomorrow?"

Dr. V shook his head. "I need you to ride the best race of your life on Saturday. Potential sponsors will be here, watching. If you put forth a solid effort, I will have some sent out to him that same day via special courier. It will cost me plenty, but he will have it by Sunday, one week from today."

"That might be too late! He needs it *before* the race."

"Sorry. This is the best I can do. Your home telephone was bugged, you know, and I overheard him and PawPaw saying that a person can last one lunar cycle without it. He should be fine."

I glared at Dr. V.

"I see that you are upset," he said. "Do you need time to think it over?"

"There isn't any time."

"I'll leave that decision to you. Now, I need you to empty your pockets. Place the contents on the table."

I was confused. Why was the headlamp charger such a big deal? I pulled it from my pocket and put it on the table.

Dr. V rolled his eyes. "Your other pocket, Phoenix."

"It's empty."

"Is it?"

I put my hand into my other pocket, and my eyes widened. I pulled out the glass test tube that Hú Dié had filled with dragon bone earlier.

"Your cousin—sorry, your *girlfriend*—slipped that into your pocket while she was squeezing the life out of you," Dr. V said. "My best guess is that she planned to hide your unconscious body and leave you to wake on your own and make a break for it solo, using that head-lamp to light your way. What a considerate young lady."

I scowled. "She's not my girlfriend."

Dr. V laughed. "No? Then why are you so quick to deny it?"

I didn't reply.

"It's okay, Phoenix," Dr. V said. "I never did believe that she was your cousin, and I'm glad you have no strong attraction to her. It will make things easier for you."

"What do you plan to do with her?"

"Like I said, I could use more guinea pigs. I believe I'll start with her."

"You can't do that!"

"Sure I can. People would come looking for you, but not her. I'll just lock her up somewhere quiet. Visitors come to the United States from all over the world, only to disappear. They are called defectors. If anyone is suspicious of me, I will grant them full access to search this facility. I guarantee she will have been moved by then."

I glanced at Hú Dié and saw that she was staring at Bjorn's lifeless body. She had fear in her eyes.

I shook my head at Dr. V. "If you want me to ride for you, you have to promise to not give Hú Dié any dragon bone."

Hú Dié glanced at me. She seemed surprised and moved by my request.

"Fine," Dr. V replied. "So, we have a deal?"

I thought for a moment. "One more condition."

Dr. V cocked an eyebrow. "A negotiator? Okay. What else do you want?"

"I want to call my grandfather in a few hours, after he wakes up."

"You can call your grandfather, sure," Dr. V said, "but you mustn't share the terms of our arrangement just yet. You may only inquire about his health. I will allow you to call your grandfather again in a few days in order to discuss the dragon bone. Do we have a deal?"

I reluctantly nodded. "We have a deal."

24

I was restless. I lay in bed in my Team Vanderhausen room, but sleep wouldn't come. The incident in the lab and my recent long nap saw to that. Murphy drilling and pounding outside Hú Dié's door down the corridor didn't help, either. I checked the clock. It said 4:10 a.m.

I climbed out of bed and turned on the light. Maybe a little exercise would help. I could tire myself out on the equipment in the training room, then try to get some sleep. I dressed, wishing my team riding kit had arrived. I had a feeling I was going to be on the saddle awhile. I considered putting on the custom padded riding shorts that Hú Dié had sewn for me, but I wanted nothing to do with anything made by her.

I opened my door and saw Murphy attaching a large gate latch and keyed padlock to the outside of Hú Dié's door. She wasn't going anywhere. I wasn't, either, but I tried not to think about it. I needed to remain here, for Grandfather's sake.

I ignored Murphy as I left my room, and he ignored me. I hoped he had a huge headache from Lin Tan pistol-whipping him. I walked through the dining and kitchen areas, then into the training room, flipping on lights along the way. I stopped to check one of the stationary trainers, spinning its resistance wheel and verifying that its rear-wheel supporters were assembled and ready to go. I had toyed with a few different models in bike shops before, and it looked to me like everything on this unit was operational except for the fancy computer projection equipment. I didn't need that, anyway.

I headed out of the training room, down the long corridor, and into the workshop. I grabbed the bike that I had ridden against Ryan and took it back to the training room, where I connected its rear wheel axle to the unit I had inspected. Next, I went into the dining area and found four empty water bottles on one of the shelves. I filled the bottles from a fancy water cooler and went back into the training area, placing one of the water bottles into the bottle cage on the bike frame. I put the other bottles on the floor within easy reach.

I climbed onto the bike and began to spin. I started with an easy gear to warm up my legs, and then I shifted through increasingly difficult gears until I had run out of large sprockets. I rode the bike's most difficult gear combination for more than an hour before I began to feel even remotely tired.

It was going to take forever for me to purge the negative energy that had built up inside me.

At the two-hour mark, I heard someone heading my way through the dining area. I flung sheets of sweat from my brow and looked over at the double doors as Dr. V stepped through them. He was dressed in a team riding kit.

"Need to burn off a little steam?" Dr. V asked. "I don't blame you."

I didn't reply. I began to pedal faster.

Dr. V grinned. "Go ahead, let it out. I use my bike to help me relieve my frustrations, too. I'm heading out on my morning ride now. Ryan will be joining me. I suggest you behave yourself. Murphy has finished his work inside, but he is watching your every move from his camper. If he sees anything suspicious, he'll be here in a flash with that huge revolver of his."

I said nothing.

"See you in an hour or so," Dr. V said, and he left the way he'd come. Ryan walked past me a few moments later without so much as a glance.

I continued riding at a hard pace until Dr. V eventually poked his head through the double doors again. His face was slick with sweat and road grime. "I'm back," he said. "I'm going to shower off in one of the rooms. Ryan is still out riding."

Dr. V left again, and I glanced at the floor. There was a huge puddle of sweat beneath my bike, and all of my water bottles were empty. I'd never ridden this hard before. I kept at it, though, and after another twenty minutes, my legs began to cramp.

That was it. I was toast. I crawled off the bike and wobbled on rubbery legs into the dining area to get a drink. There I found Dr. V mixing ingredients for a shake in one of the blenders. His hair was damp from his shower, and he was wearing a different riding kit. The man seriously needed to expand his wardrobe.

"Care for a protein shake?" he asked. "It's my own special recipe."

I looked at the counter and saw several banana peels and an open can of cocoa alongside several open containers of various powdered supplements. Banana-chocolate shakes were my favorite. I hadn't eaten since yesterday afternoon and was hungry as well as thirsty.

I looked at my watch. It was early, and Grandfather probably wouldn't be awake, but I wanted to try to reach him. Dr. V owed me a phone call.

"I'd like to call my grandfather first, like you promised," I said. "Then I'll have a shake."

"Do you think this is a good time?"

"It's perfect."

"Okay. Just a minute." Dr. V put the lid on the blender jar and pushed a button on the machine's base. The blender roared to life, then stopped a few seconds later. Dr. V removed the jar and poured the shake into two glasses, which he set on one of the tables. "Let's have a seat."

I sat on the opposite side of the table from him. He

pulled a cell phone from one of the large outer pockets sewn into the back of his riding jersey and tapped a few buttons. He pushed the phone over to me. "You'll use this phone instead of the facility's landline. I just set the speakerphone. All you have to do is dial the number and hit *send*."

I dialed the number. It rang five times before someone picked up.

"Hello?"

I felt an unexpected surge of relief. It was great to hear a familiar voice. "Hi, Uncle Tí. It's Phoenix."

"Phoenix!" Uncle Tí said. "Where are you?"

Dr. V grabbed my arm and shook his head. He clearly didn't want me to tell my uncle anything.

I ignored Uncle Tí's question. "How is Grandfather? Can I talk to him?"

Uncle Tí took a deep breath. "I'm sorry, Phoenix, but you can't. He's slipped into some kind of coma. You need to come home."

"What! When did this happen?"

"Yesterday. He told me to expect it to happen, but he didn't anticipate it occurring so soon."

I felt tears begin to trickle down my cheeks. They mixed with the sweat that was still streaming from my forehead. "I *have* to talk with him! It's not fair. I'm trying my best."

"I know you are," Uncle Tí said. "No one is doubting you. I'm doing my best, too. These things happen."

"How much longer do you think he has?"

"I don't know. I have no experience with his condition. He thought he would be okay if I could administer the . . . um, herb before Tuesday."

I looked pleadingly at Dr. V.

Dr. V picked up one of the shake glasses and casually took a sip. He shook his head again.

I hammered my fist on the tabletop. My shake nearly toppled off the table, and I grabbed the cold, heavy glass.

"Are you okay?" Uncle Tí asked.

I fought to speak through my tears. No words came.

"Where are you?" Uncle Tí asked again. "My caller ID says it's an unavailable number. Give me your phone number and I'll call you back in a few hours. You need time to digest all of this."

Rage began to burn deep inside my skull. Sweat cascaded into my watery eyes, and I raised the cold shake glass to my face in an effort to cool myself down. The rim of the glass brushed against my nose, and I caught the scent of something familiar.

Something old.

Something ancient.

I felt Dr. V's gaze upon me, and I glared at him. He seemed amused. I sniffed the contents of the glass one more time, and the rage in my head exploded into a supernova.

"Phoenix?" Uncle Tí said over the phone. "Phoenix! Are you there?"

I hit the phone's END button and slammed the heavy glass down on the tabletop. I stared at Dr. V. "You put dragon bone in this."

Dr. V grinned and reached behind his back. He

pulled a stoppered glass test tube from one of his jersey pockets. The tube was full of grayish powder, and he shook it in my face; then he returned the tube to his pocket. "For the past week, I've been consuming it. Protein shakes seem to mask the taste better than anything else I've tried. I have to admit, dragon bone tastes horrible. Here's to my expanding fortune—*and* immortality!"

Dr. V raised the heavy glass to his lips, and a quote came to my mind, one that is often used in the cycling world but actually came from Indy car racing legend Rick Mears: *To finish first, you must first finish.* Grandfather was going to die while this cheating, thieving mad scientist sat in front of me, consuming the very substance necessary to keep Grandfather alive. What I was doing here—serving as a puppet in order to receive weekly dragon bone rations for Grandfather—wasn't finishing. It was quitting, and quitting was worse than losing.

I *hate* to lose.

I dove across the table, driving the heel of my palm into the base of Dr. V's upturned drinking glass. Dr. V choked and the bridge of his nose snapped as the thick glass rammed into his face. Blood squirted down to his chest and he toppled backward in his chair, his head bouncing off the dining area's tile floor.

I scrambled off the table and stood. Dr. V didn't move. For an instant, I thought I had killed him, and I began to panic. But then I saw his chest rising and falling, and I knew he had just slipped into unconsciousness. Like Grandfather.

I flipped Dr. V over and reached into his jersey pockets. The test tube filled with dragon bone had smashed, but I found a set of keys. I took the keys, grabbed his cell phone, and headed for the lab.

I reached the corridor leading to the lab and saw that, thankfully, Murphy was gone. I paused before Hú Dié's door. Although she had used me, I couldn't leave her here. Besides, if Murphy really was keeping an eye on the security cameras, her fighting skills would come in handy. Murphy might be back here any moment.

I flipped through the keys and found a shiny small one that looked newer than the rest. I tried it in the padlock affixed to the gate latch on Hú Dié's door, and the key worked perfectly. I swung the door open and called out, "Hú Dié! Let's go!"

"Huh?" Hú Dié mumbled in a groggy tone.

I switched on the light and hurried over to her bed. I grabbed her by the wrist and shouted, "Come on! We have to fight!"

Hú Dié tensed at the word *fight,* and I let go of her arm. I jumped back as a *whoosh* of air blasted past my head. It was her elbow.

"Don't fight *me,* you idiot!" I said. "We might have to fight Murphy. We're going to escape. Hurry!"

Hú Dié seemed to come to her senses, and she rolled out of bed. She was still wearing what she had on earlier. She pulled her pink mountain biking shoes out of a suitcase. "We're going to ride out of here, right?"

"Yeah."

She put her riding shoes on and stuffed her passport in her pocket. "Where is Dr. V?"

"Out cold on the dining room floor."

"Ouch."

We stopped before the locked lab door. I began to fumble with the keys. Hú Dié looked at me and said, "I am truly sorry about what happened earlier."

"Whatever," I replied without looking at her. I selected a key and inserted it into the lock. The door opened on the first try. We hurried inside and closed the door behind us. I flipped on the lights.

Hú Dié shrieked. "Ryan!"

Ryan was lying shirtless and still as a stone atop the stainless-steel table. Dozens of wires ran from machines to his forehead and chest.

Hú Dié raced to his side. "Ryan! Wake up!"

Ryan didn't budge.

I hurried over to him and Hú Dié.

"He's not dead, is he?" Hú Dié asked. "I can see his chest moving like he's breathing."

"I think he's just asleep," I replied. "He went riding with Dr. V this morning and must have come back here for tests or something. Dr. V lied and said he was still out on his bike."

"Dr. V lying, imagine that."

A muscle twitched in Ryan's abdomen, just below his belly button.

"Hey!" Hú Dié said. "Did you see that? It was right over his *dan tien*—his chi center."

I nodded. "That's where a person's life energy is supposedly stored. Maybe dragon bone somehow connects with a person's chi."

"I *know* what a *dan tien* is," Hú Dié said. "It's also your absolute center of gravity and the spot where you feel butterflies—*Hú Dié*—in your stomach. Should we try and wake him? Or maybe tie him up so he can't get in our way?"

"We probably couldn't wake him if we wanted to. We need to just go. We can call the police or something later."

I spotted the dragon bone vessels and ran over to them. They were still sitting empty on the same counter. Hú Dié's hydration pack was also on the counter, as was the silk drawstring bag. I opened the bag and found that it was filled with pure white powder. It had no grayish tint. I stared at it.

"Come on!" Hú Dié said. "Grab the dragon bone."

I raised my nose to the bag and sniffed. There was no odor. I looked at Hú Dié. "This isn't dragon bone."

"Arrgh!" she said. "Of course it isn't. Dr. V wouldn't be stupid enough to leave it out in plain sight in those dragon-shaped containers. It was a trick." She glanced at the wall of two-way mirrors and the door with the key-pad. "I bet he keeps it in there."

I ran to the door and tried the handle. "Locked," I said.

Hú Dié howled and ran toward the mirrors. I jumped back as she threw both of her arms over her head, then slammed them into the section of mirrors closest to the door.

The entire section exploded. Pieces of thick, mirrored safety glass sailed in every direction. Hú Dié's momentum was so great that she tumbled headlong into the other room.

I rushed over and poked my head into the space beyond. Hú Dié was on the ground, covered in safety glass.

"Are you okay?" I asked.

She stood and nodded, shaking the pieces from her clothes.

"That was awesome," I said.

Hú Dié grinned weakly. "That kind of hurt. Grab the silk bag and backpack and get in here."

I retrieved the bag and dumped the contents into a trash bin beside the counter. The powder looked like it might be baking soda. I turned the bag inside out so that whatever it was wouldn't contaminate the dragon bone; then I grabbed the backpack. Hú Dié turned on the lights inside Dr. V's office, and she tried to open the door to the lab from the inside. It worked.

I ran into the office, prepared to tear it apart, but that wasn't necessary. There were several large glass vials containing grayish powder on a shelf above Dr. V's cyclocross bike, which was leaning against the wall.

"There," I said, pointing to the shelf. I pulled down one of the vials, popped the top, and took a whiff. "We did it," I said. "Help me pour these into the bag."

"Are you sure you trust me?" Hú Dié asked.

"No. But do it, anyway."

Hú Dié lowered her eyes and got to work. We finished transferring the dragon bone to the bag; then she walked out of the office to take one last look at Ryan while I put the bag into the backpack.

I slung the pack over my shoulders. "Are you ready?"

Hú Dié didn't reply. I heard a door open.

I walked out of the office, expecting to see her heading out of the lab. Instead, I saw Murphy. The tall, wiry Texan raised his massive revolver and leveled it at my chest.

"Fixin' to go somewhere?" he drawled.

25

I stared across Dr. V's lab at the gaping barrel of Murphy's gun. He stepped into the lab with his revolver raised, and I caught a blur of movement out of the corner of my eye.

It was Hú Dié. She had been hiding, pressed up against the inner wall of the lab, near the door. She let loose one of her banshee wails, and her iron forearms slammed down onto Murphy's gun arm. I heard bones crunch. The gun hit the floor with a clatter, and Murphy's pain-filled grunt was cut short by a dull thud as Hú Dié cracked him on the temple with a hammer fist. Murphy crumpled to the ground, but his eyes remained half-open.

"Get something to tie him with!" Hú Dié said. "Quickly! He's still semiconscious."

The only thing I saw that might do the job was the wires connected to Ryan. I ran over to him and tore every last one free from the adhesive pads attached to his chest and forehead.

Ryan stirred and opened his eyes for a moment, then closed them again. I held my breath, watching him closely. The muscles above his *dan tien* twitched a few times, but other than that, his breathing was regular.

"Phoenix, hurry!" Hú Dié said.

I yanked the long wires free from the machines in a flurry of sparks and took the wires to Hú Dié. Together we tied up Murphy. When we'd finished, we rushed into the dining area and saw that Dr. V was still unconscious.

"Should we tie him up, too?" Hú Dié asked.

"Might as well," I said. "Better safe than sorry."

Hú Dié yanked the power cord from the base of the blender and tied Dr. V's hands behind his back while I went into the training area and disconnected my bike from the stationary trainer. We ran down the long corridor to the workshop and were greeted with a disturbing sight. Someone had moved Lin Tan and Bjorn's pickup truck into the shop. There was a lumpy tarp draped over the pickup's bed, and it took little imagination to guess what lay beneath it.

Neither Hú Dié nor I said a word. We just grabbed new helmets from the shelves and strapped the lids onto our heads. Hú Dié lowered the seat on Ryan's bike and climbed on.

"Aren't you going to adjust the handlebars, too?" I asked.

She leaned forward and checked the fit. "These are

close enough. I want to get out of here. I'm going to have nightmares for the rest of my life."

"Will your shoe brackets connect with that type of pedal?"

"Yes. I'm good."

I leaned my bike against the workbench and walked over to the roll-up bay door that led to the outside. I started flipping through keys, and Hú Dié said, "It's a little gold one. I watched Murphy lock up before we went to Austin. There are actually two locks, one on each side of the door, but they use the same key."

I found the key and opened the locks; then I pressed a garage door opener button mounted to the wall. A motor moaned and creaked to life overhead, and the door began to rise, letting in the morning sun. I was about to head for my bike when I heard a low growl outside.

I looked back to see Murphy's dog, Bones.

"Oh, crap," Hú Dié said.

"Nice doggy?" I said.

The big dog growled again, and I saw the hairs on the back of his neck rise.

I didn't move a muscle.

"You didn't happen to grab anything from Murphy, did you?" Hú Dié asked.

"No," I replied, trying to keep my voice calm and even. "And it's probably a good thing I didn't. Remember how Murphy said his dog didn't like people messing with his property? But I wouldn't mind holding his gun right now."

"I hid the gun up high in one of the wall cabinets

while you were getting the wires. He'll never find it. We tied him up, though. Do you think the dog can smell his scent on us?"

"I don't know, and I don't plan on getting close enough to him to find out."

The door stopped, fully open, and Bones took several steps toward me. The dog sniffed the air. His eyes narrowed.

I took a step backward, and the dog began to bark ferociously.

"Bones!" a voice suddenly drawled from within the training facility. "Here, boy!"

Bones stopped barking and tilted his head as if listening.

"Bones!" Murphy hollered again from the lab. His voice was faint but clear. "Here, boy! Here, boy!"

Bones yowled and raced toward his master's voice. The dog shot through the open door leading to the long corridor and was out of sight.

I grabbed my bike and adjusted the pack on my back; then I looked at Hú Dié. "We'd better jet."

She nodded.

I jammed my feet into my pedal cages and heard Murphy holler, "Yee-haw! Chew me loose, boy! We're goin' huntin'!"

I blasted out of the workshop with Hú Dié riding close behind, and my fatigued legs immediately reminded me that I had just ridden hard for hours on the stationary trainer. My body wasn't pleased.

"Which way?" Hú Dié asked.

"Cross-country," I replied, heading for the cyclocross course. "If Bones can chew half as strong as Murphy claims, Murphy will be in his truck in minutes. He would catch us on the ranch road before we even reached the gate."

"Can a hunting dog follow the scent of bike tires?"

"I don't know, but I have a feeling we're going to see soon enough. Stay close."

I reached the cyclocross course and followed it for a few hundred yards; then I left the course and plowed straight into dry ankle-high grass, making a beeline for the hills. The uneven ground turned my fully rigid cyclocross bike into a bucking bronco, but I managed to stay in the saddle. I glanced back at Hú Dié and saw that she was keeping pace, which was good. I also saw a small cloud of dust rushing toward us from the training facility, which was bad.

It was Bones.

I feathered my brakes, slowing slightly. "Hú Dié," I said, "Bones is coming. You go on ahead, into the hills. I'll try to lose him."

"Are you crazy?" she replied. "You can't outrun that dog over this ground. You probably couldn't even do it on smooth pavement. He's huge."

"I've got to do *something*. He's going to run us down, anyway. Get out of here, now! He can only chase one of us, and I want it to be me. I'm the stronger sprinter and you know it."

Hú Dié huffed her disapproval, but she picked up her pace. I slowed further.

I'd been chased by unleashed dogs more times than I could count while riding on mountain bike trails, and I knew that road bikers who favored back roads in rural areas had it even worse. Defensive strategies included everything from handlebar-mounted cans of pepper spray to squirting dogs in the eyes with your water bottle. I had neither, so I decided to try a trick that had saved my ankles on more than one occasion.

I shifted to an easy gear and kept my pace steady, allowing Bones to get an accurate sense of my speed as I pedaled ahead of him. When the dog neared, he began to bay as if he were hot on the trail of a rabid raccoon. I concentrated, mentally calling up what little energy reserves I had left.

Bones opened his jaws wide, and I fought the urge to kick him in the face. That would be like sticking my foot into the mouth of a hungry lion. Instead, the instant I sensed the dog was about to snap his jaws shut, I hammered with all my might.

I sprinted forward, my abrupt change in speed throwing off Bones's attack. The dog's jaws closed on thin air, and he stumbled. Unfortunately, he didn't go down like most dogs do. The seasoned hunting dog regained his footing and began to pick up speed.

I realized I didn't stand a chance. My exhausted legs were already beginning to give out. I looked ahead toward Hú Dié and saw that she was turning around.

"What are you doing?" I shouted.

She didn't answer. She completed her turn and began to hammer in my direction. I glanced back and saw that

Bones was nearly upon me, even though I was still riding fairly fast.

"Cut hard to your right on three!" Hú Dié cried.

I looked up and saw that she, too, was coming straight at me. She reached down and grabbed the emergency tire pump that was attached to the down tube of Ryan's bike. The pump was roughly the size and shape of a nightstick.

"One!" Hú Dié shouted. "Two! *Three!*"

I cut my wheel hard to the right, and Hú Dié barreled past me just inches away on my left. She swung the tire pump down with her left hand, whacking the dog hard across his hips before it could clamp down on me.

Bones stumbled in a tangle of legs, dust, and fur before tumbling end over end, as Hú Dié slammed on her brakes.

I turned my bike around and headed for Hú Dié. I watched in horror as Bones jumped to his feet and began to stalk toward her. The dog was snarling viciously, lines of saliva cascading from his jowls.

Hú Dié climbed off Ryan's bike and crouched behind it, holding the bike in front of her like a shield. She switched the tire pump to her right hand, raising it like a club. Was she actually going to war with this huge dog?

I heard a piercing whistle in the distance, and Bones froze in his tracks. I looked toward the training facility and saw a massive cloud of dust heading our way. I also heard hooves pounding against the dry earth.

"Murphy is coming!" I shouted to Hú Dié. "He's riding Theo!"

Hú Dié glanced back toward Murphy, while Bones remained still as a statue, his eyes locked on Hú Dié as though she were a treed opossum.

Murphy approached, and I saw that he held a length of rope in one hand. He began to swing the rope over his head, and a loop formed in midair. He was planning to lasso us like stray calves.

I considered what I knew about horses and bicycles. On multi-use trails, bikers were legally required to yield to horses because horses were instinctually prey animals. To a horse, a bicycle racing toward it was no different from a bear or wolf.

I was still pedaling, so I steered toward Theo and willed my legs to give me all they could. As I neared the horse, Theo's black eyes widened with terror. Murphy tossed aside his lasso and gripped the horse's reins with both hands, and I rose out of my own saddle, pulling up and back on the handlebars.

My front wheel lifted into the air a few feet from Theo, and the horse lost his mind. He reared up on his back legs, pawing at the air with his powerful front hooves. Murphy was tossed from his saddle, the reins slipping from his hands. I shifted my weight forward and leaned to the side, slamming my front wheel back down to the ground while swerving around the frightened animal. I managed to hold my line without falling off the bike.

I looked back and saw that Murphy had landed on a pile of rocks, probably headfirst. It didn't look as if he would be getting up anytime soon. That was what he got for not wearing a helmet.

Bones yelped and ran over to his master as I headed for Hú Dié. Theo bolted into the hills.

Hú Dié climbed back onto Ryan's bike and was clipping into the pedals when I reached her.

"That was genius!" she said.

I nodded. "You weren't so bad yourself. I guess I owe you one."

"Not a chance. I am so far in the hole with you, I might never see the light of day. I—" She stopped in midsentence and stared toward the training facility parking lot. "I don't believe it. Murphy must have woken Dr. V and cut him loose."

I turned and saw a black SUV lurching over the uneven ground toward us. I felt a welcome burst of adrenaline. My weary legs were going to need it. "Follow me!" I said. "I think I know a way to lose him."

I rode hard back toward the cyclocross course, reaching it near the first hill with Hú Dié at my side. We blasted over the hill together and cruised along until I saw what I was looking for—the narrow side trail I'd noticed when I'd raced against Ryan. I hoped it would be too narrow for the SUV.

I turned onto the trail, and Hú Dié asked, "Where does this lead?"

"I have no idea."

"Do you have that GPS unit with you?"

"No. It wouldn't help us, anyway. It only contained maps of China."

Hú Dié cursed, and I heard an engine roar.

"We should split up!" Hú Dié called out. "You stay on the trail."

"No!" I said. "*You* stay on the trail. I'll risk going off-road."

Hú Dié began to argue, but I pulled off the trail first. I raced parallel to her for a bit to see what Dr. V would do, when suddenly Hú Dié screamed and went sailing through the air over her handlebars. It was as though an invisible force field had stopped her bike while she continued forward.

I cut my wheel hard to the right and slammed on my brakes, skidding sideways over the packed ground. I pulled my right foot free of its pedal cage and rammed my heel into the earth, bringing my rear tire around 180 degrees so that I was now sliding backward.

BOOM!

My rear tire exploded upon impact with a barbed-wire fence that I didn't see but guessed was there because of what had happened to Hú Dié. My bike came to an abrupt halt, but I managed to keep myself clear of the fence.

I stepped out of the other pedal cage and threw the bike down, then carefully slipped between strands of wire that were obscured by a row of scrub trees and bushes. On the other side of the fencerow was an enormous farm field. I could see towering irrigation equipment and mile after mile of waist-high green plants. I ran to Hú Dié, who was lying on a bed of what I supposed were soybeans.

She groaned and sat up. "What happened?"

"You hit a barbed-wire fence," I replied. "I didn't see it, either, until I was right on top of it. Did you break anything? Are you cut?"

Hú Dié quickly looked herself over. "I'm fine." She patted one of the dense green plants beside her. "These really helped cushion my fall. The earth here is nice and soft, too. Is Dr. V—"

The approaching roar of the SUV's engine answered any questions about the location of the black truck. I watched through the fencerow as the vehicle cruised parallel to the fence before reaching a gap between two trees and crashing through. The SUV turned toward us and tore across the farmland, moist clumps of soil churning up from beneath the truck's knobby four-wheel-drive tires.

I ripped the pack from my back and pulled out the shimmering silk bag of dragon bone. I stepped in front of Hú Dié and held the bag before me like a talisman.

Dr. V slammed on the SUV's brakes, and the truck slid over the slick vegetation before stopping thirty feet from Hú Dié and me. He leaped out with his rifle raised.

I glanced over at Hú Dié and heard a shout: "IT'S PAYBACK TIME!"

I turned back to Dr. V, but he was no longer looking in our direction, and I realized that he hadn't spoken.

It was Ryan.

The big kid was racing toward us all atop Dr. V's cyclocross bike. He was shirtless, but he wore a helmet and riding shoes. He had crossed through the gap in the fence made by Dr. V's SUV.

As Ryan bore down, he roared like a lion. I prepared to leap to my left to avoid his charge when, inexplicably, he veered right. I watched in utter confusion as Ryan plowed straight into Dr. V. The force of the impact knocked Dr. V flat onto his back, sending the rifle sailing into the tree line. Ryan had already unclipped his feet from the pedals, and as he ditched the moving bike on top of his uncle, the chain slipped off. However, the bike's pedals and large drive sprocket continued to spin, digging into the side of Dr. V's head and leaving him unconscious in a pool of blood.

Ryan's momentum kept him sailing forward until he slammed into the ground. Hú Dié and I rushed to his side, and I expected to find him out cold, but instead he was thrashing about, clawing at his bare abdomen. He was shivering despite the warm morning air, and the flesh across his *dan tien* was undulating wildly, as though something were attempting to crawl out of his body. His eyes were blurry and his gaze was unfocused, but he managed to turn his head toward me and gasp, "Phoenix, make it stop. Please."

26

"Hang in there, Ryan," I said. "We'll get help."

Ryan took several deep breaths, his stomach still spasming.

"This is bad," Hú Dié said.

I glanced over at Dr. V. Amazingly, he was still breathing.

"We need to call 911," I said. I pulled Dr. V's cell phone from my pocket and made the call, describing the facility's location as best I could with Ryan's help. The dispatcher said it would be twenty minutes before help arrived, because our location was fairly remote. I thanked her and hung up.

Ryan looked at his uncle, then looked away. "Is he going to make it?"

"I don't know," I replied. "Dragon bone is mysterious stuff. You do know he was taking it, right?"

"Yeah."

Hú Dié stood. "We should go back to the facility before the police and ambulances arrive, Phoenix. Maybe you should wait here, Ryan."

Ryan shook his head. "I'd rather not be alone right now."

"What about your uncle?" I asked.

"I don't think he's going anywhere. Besides, we can't do anything for him. I also need to open the front gate. My uncle has a hidden switch in his office that's difficult to describe." Ryan grunted and stood, his stomach roiling as though it was cramping and uncramping. He was tough. He began to jog quickly, but in an awkward, hunched-over posture, clutching his stomach.

I shoved the silk bag filled with dragon bone into the backpack, and Hú Dié and I chased after Ryan. When we caught up with him, I said, "Thanks a million, Ryan. We owe you big-time."

"No," Ryan replied. "My uncle needed to be stopped. I had no idea how crazy he was until I watched him shoot Lin Tan and Bjorn."

"You saw that?" Hú Dié asked. "How?"

"I hacked the security camera system. My Internet connection is on the same feed."

"But Phoenix said you were asleep."

"I was, until you guys woke me without knowing it. There is a silent alarm on the door to my uncle's lab that alerts his home computer, as well as his cell phone. I hacked that, too, and set an alarm of my own to wake me if you guys broke in there. I figured you would at least try. I would have done the same thing."

"I didn't know you were a hacker," I said.

"There is a lot you don't know about me."

I nodded. "I guess you're right. Maybe I'll get a chance to find out once we get back home? I'm really sorry Jake and I never invited you over to hang out. The truth is, I've always been embarrassed about how small my house is. No one besides Jake has ever seen it."

"Really?"

"Yeah. There is something else I should probably tell you, too. After your dad passed away, Jake and I didn't know what to say to you anymore, so we said nothing. Stupid, I know. I apologize."

"Thanks for telling me," Ryan said. "I appreciate it."

"Thanks for listening," I replied. "Things are going to change between us, I promise. That is, if you still want to be my friend."

Ryan smiled. "I'd like that."

"Maybe we could do some training rides together," I offered.

Ryan's smile faded. "I don't think so."

"Why not?"

"The security cameras have audio. I heard my uncle say that I'll never be a great rider. Maybe he's right. I can't beat you, even when I try cheating with a powerful substance. I'm done."

"Listen," Hú Dié said, "I hardly know you, but I can tell that you're not the type of person who gives up easily. Forget what he said. I also know a lot about riders, and you're *good*. We'll get your stomach sorted out, and you'll be winning races, I promise."

"You think?" Ryan asked.

"Definitely," I said. "*My* uncle can probably help with your dragon bone situation. My grandfather can help, too, if we can get him some more dragon bone in time."

Ryan glanced at the pack on my back. "You have it, don't you? I was only pretending to be asleep on that metal table in the lab. I heard everything, and I saw some of it, too." He turned to Hú Dié. "That was great, the way you took out Murphy."

Hú Dié grinned. "He had it coming."

"Speaking of Murphy," I said, slowing down. "Look."

We reached the spot where Murphy had fallen off his horse. There was some blood on the rock pile, but there was no sign of him or Bones.

"Keep your eyes peeled," I said, and we continued on.

We got to the training facility and saw that, thankfully, Murphy's truck was gone. We hurried through the open workshop door, past Lin Tan and Bjorn's pickup, and on to the lab. The lab door was open, and we rushed inside. Ryan went into Dr. V's office and popped a hidden panel inside a desk drawer.

"That's strange," Ryan said as he flipped the switch to open the gate. "I thought the switch would have already been flipped by Murphy since he is gone—"

The outer side door to Dr. V's office suddenly burst open and Murphy strolled in, a different pistol held out in front of him. I rushed for the main lab door and heard claws scrambling down the corridor. Bones was coming from that direction, boxing us in. The dog bared his fangs and leaped at me, and I swung the door with all my might. It latched closed an instant before the animal slammed against it, snarling. Bones began to howl.

"Now he's really not going to like you, Phoenix," Murphy said. "If you behave, I'll be sure to kill you before I let him rip you to shreds. Go stand in the center of the lab. All of you."

Ryan left the office and joined me in the middle of the lab, but Hú Dié didn't budge from her position near the stainless-steel table.

Murphy walked out of the office, into the lab. "Move it, Hú Dié," he said.

She looked over at me and said, "I'm sorry for the way I treated you." I saw her eyes turn cold.

"Hú Dié, no!" I said, but it was too late. She lunged at Murphy's gun, which was pointed at me.

Hú Dié gripped the small weapon with her right hand, completely covering the front of the short barrel, and Murphy fired.

CRACK!

Hú Dié shrieked and flung her arm aside, tearing the gun from Murphy's grasp and hurling it across the room. I made a move for it as Murphy reached behind his back and pulled a large hunting knife from a sheath. Hú Dié froze, blood dripping from her hand.

Murphy glared at her. "You're hard as nails, young lady," he said. "I almost feel bad about doing this." He raised his knife.

BANG!

A shot from a larger gun rang out from overhead.

BANG! BANG!

All three bullets connected with Murphy. He stumbled forward before collapsing. He wouldn't be getting back up.

I looked up to see a blue tarp covering the broken skylight. Lin Tan was peering through a slit in the tarp. He pushed the tarp aside and aimed the pistol at me.

"Where is it?" he hissed.

"Where is what?" I replied.

"You know *what*. The dragon bone."

"I don't know what you're talking about—"

Sirens began to wail in the distance. Lots of sirens.

Lin Tan aimed the gun at Ryan. "Get me the keys to your dad's motorcycle, or you and your friends are dead. Hurry up."

Ryan retrieved the keys from Dr. V's desk and threw them up to Lin Tan. As he caught them, I noticed a large, crude bandage was strapped over his shoulder.

Lin Tan saw me staring at his wound from Dr. V's rifle. "It's not that bad," he said. "At least I survived, unlike Bjorn. You and I will see each other again, I promise." He looked at Hú Dié and asked in Chinese, *"Gen wo lai?"* "Come with me?"

She shook her head. *"Bu yao, xie xie."* "No, thanks."

I smiled.

Lin Tan shrugged and disappeared. A moment later, I heard the motorcycle tear off toward the cyclocross course and, I was guessing, the bean field beyond. Considering the path Dr. V had undoubtedly cut with his

SUV, Lin Tan would make it through on that big motorcycle. He would be long gone before we could tell the authorities what had happened.

I ran over to Hú Dié, and Ryan hurried to close the office door that led outside.

"I want to keep Bones out," Ryan explained. "In case he leaves the corridor and comes around to this side of the building."

"Good thinking," I said.

As the sirens grew closer, I took Hú Dié's injured hand and we sat down on the floor. Neither of us spoke. There was a lot of blood, and I had to force myself not to retch. From what I could tell, Murphy's small bullet had passed clean through the webbing between her thumb and index finger, and some skin had been burned by the heat of the barrel. With luck, she would be fine. Her whole body was trembling now, probably from shock.

Ryan left the office and crossed the lab. He opened a set of blinds. We saw three police cars arrive, along with two ambulances. One of the squad cars drove around back, and a few moments later, Bones began to howl from the corridor. The officers must have come into the facility through the shop because someone shouted, "Secure that dog before we go any farther!"

I suddenly remembered the dragon bone and scrambled to my feet. I flipped through the cabinets, looking for a place to hide it, and found three large plastic containers of protein powder. I hurriedly dumped the protein powder down a lab sink, then rinsed and dried the containers before refilling them with the dragon bone. I put the containers back into the cabinet and quickly rinsed the empty bag before throwing it, soaking wet, into the trash bin where I'd dumped the fake dragon bone powder.

Someone tried turning the knob on the locked lab door, and I ran over to it.

"Is the coast clear?" I called out.

"Clear!" was the answer from the other side.

I slowly opened the door and found two officers standing there. I'd never been so happy to see strangers in all my life.

"My friend has been shot!" I said. "Please, hurry!"

I rushed back to Hú Dié. She was still shaking. I leaned close to her and whispered, "You saved my life. I don't know how to thank you."

Her teeth began to chatter and she punched me with her good hand. Hard. "I warned you before—stop saying 'thank you' so much!"

27

It was difficult, but over the coming days I managed not to give Hú Dié a single thank-you. However, I didn't hold back with anyone else—from the officers who came to our rescue and added our mostly true statements to their official reports; to the emergency medical technicians who patched up Hú Dié's hand; to Ryan's mother, who flew out that day and brought us back to Indiana with the dragon bone on her chartered plane; to my uncle Tí, who was letting me and Hú Dié stay with him, as well as providing Ryan with ongoing treatment to try to sever his connection with dragon bone.

More than that, Uncle Tí had revived Grandfather.

I was teaching Grandfather's tai chi class at the nursing home several days after our return, when my uncle interrupted and told me that Grandfather had regained consciousness. I rushed to his room, leaving Uncle Tí to finish the lesson.

"Phoenix," Grandfather whispered in a dry, raspy voice when I entered. "You did it. *Xie xie*—thank you."

I hurried to his side and felt tears begin to pool in the corners of my eyes. This was going to be bittersweet. "Welcome back, Grandfather."

He smiled weakly. "I sense you have a lot on your mind."

I nodded.

"What is it?"

"Everything, I guess. You . . . Ryan . . ."

Grandfather pursed his parched lips. "Your uncle just told me about Ryan's uncle, Dr. V. He did not survive."

"No," I replied. "His doctors said he lost a tremendous amount of blood, but they couldn't figure out where it all went."

"He was taking dragon bone."

"Yes."

"Dragon bone does that when its host is near death. That is how it fights to survive."

"That's what Uncle Tí thought, too. We both have a lot of questions about dragon bone, you know."

"As do I. It's a mystery, even to me."

"Did Uncle Tí tell you that Ryan has been taking it?"

"Yes. I am sorry to hear it, and I wish him the best. He has seen far too much death lately. Dragon bone will only compound his troubles."

I paused. "You mentioned someone named Ying once. You said he used to mix dragon bone with snake's blood. Do you think that would help Ryan?"

"Absolutely not. Ying was reckless. That was his

nature. Ryan needs to follow your uncle's instructions only. He should never mix dragon bone with fresh blood."

I nodded. "Who was Ying? I mean, besides your former temple brother who destroyed the place you lived."

"That is a long and difficult answer. Ying was very complicated."

"What about the Five Ancestors, then? Grandmaster Long said I was among the last of them. He also said your name isn't really Chénjí Long; it's Seh—Snake. You were one of the Five Ancestors, weren't you?"

Grandfather sighed. "I do not have the strength to go into these things at the moment. I feel myself drifting away as it is. There is something far more pressing to discuss. While I hate to burden you with this now, I need to know if you have spoken with your uncle and PawPaw about the dragon bone plans I made before I slipped into unconsciousness."

I lowered my head. "Yes."

"And how do you feel about my wishes?"

"I don't like it, but I'll do it."

"You are very brave. When will you send the remaining dragon bone to PawPaw and Grandmaster Long?"

I raised my head. "Next week. I can't believe you only want to keep ten years' worth for you. Why so little?"

Grandfather took a deep breath. "By that time, you will be out of college and more than capable of taking care of yourself. I have given this much thought, and my decision is final. Promise me you will do this."

As much as it pained me, I knew I couldn't refuse. "I promise," I said, my voice quavering.

Grandfather nodded and closed his eyes. "*Xie xie,* Phoenix. Thank you from the bottom of my heart. I am tiring again, but do not fear, I am growing stronger each day. I should be my old self again in less than a month, for better or worse."

"I'll take whatever I can get," I said, half smiling, "*better or worse.* I miss you, Grandfather."

"I miss you, too." He cleared his throat, and his tone became grave. He spoke in a whisper. "I have one other thing I must demand of you."

I straightened. "Yes?"

He smiled weakly. "Enjoy yourself, Phoenix. Life is far too short."

The following Saturday, I found myself lined up with twenty other riders across a small, paved parking lot deep inside Indiana's Brown County State Park. As Grandfather had demanded, I was doing what I enjoyed most.

It was more than two weeks since the fiasco in Texas, and Hú Dié's hand was healing well. Uncle Tí was letting her stay for the remainder of her ninety-day travel visa, and once she'd found out that girls race against guys in Indiana, she wasn't about to let me race alone. Uncle Tí gave her a clean bill of health and even wrapped her hand like a prizefighter for extra protection during the race. We also persuaded Ryan to race, and Jake was already signed up. This was going to be a good one.

Hú Dié and I were positioned on one end of the starting line, nearest the trailhead. Ryan had picked a spot in the middle, while Jake was on the far end of the line, complaining because he had shown up late and consequently received a lousy starting position. He and I had spoken a few times on the phone, but this was the first time I'd seen him since I'd returned. He kept eyeballing Hú Dié, and I made a mental note to smack him after the race.

Hú Dié had done a superb job of fixing my bike and modifying it to fit her. She'd done an equally impressive job tweaking one of Ryan's cyclocross bikes to fit me. Ryan was riding his mountain bike.

The other riders and even the race officials had questioned my sanity over the decision to ride a cyclocross bike on a mountain bike trail, but I had my reasons. A few of the more uptight kids and their parents went so far as to formally complain because they thought my bike would give me some type of overall advantage, but I argued that while this was called a mountain bike race, it was technically a bike race held on a mountain biking trail. A person could ride whatever kind of bike he or she chose, including the kids who were complaining. People rode mountain bikes in cyclocross races all the time. I was simply doing the opposite. Fortunately, the officials sided with me.

The race officials took their starting positions, and I glanced over at Ryan slumped atop his mountain bike. He was lined up next to a little kid, and the kid looked nervous. It wasn't clear if the kid had the jitters because he was racing against much older riders, or if he was worried that Ryan would topple over at any moment and crush him. Ryan looked that bad.

I felt sorry for Ryan. Hú Dié and I had ridden with him over the past few days to try to help him sweat the dragon bone out of his system, including a ride on this very course. However, he was always fatigued and his condition seemed to be getting worse. My uncle Tí had resorted to giving him a small amount of dragon bone in an effort to wean him from its hold, but even that didn't seem to be helping. With luck, the adrenaline rush this race would provide might help sever at least some of the connection.

The starter pistol fired, and I hammered my feet down onto the pedals of my borrowed 'cross bike. As expected, the cyclocross bike and its large-wheeled road-bike configuration did give me an initial advantage on the smooth pavement. I smoked everyone as I blazed across the parking lot, hitting the narrow trailhead at least fifty feet ahead of my closest competitor, who I wasn't at all surprised to see was Hú Dié. My lead continued to grow as I rushed along the relatively flat opening stretch, thick stands of tall, leafy brush smacking against my cracked goggles and duct-taped face shield. Man, it felt good to be racing again. I was glad I wasn't Jake, stuck in the back of the pack and having to battle for every inch to pass a bunch of people.

I breezed through the first section, and my lead continued to increase as I approached the next section, where the trail began to open up. Massive oak trees grew thirty or more feet apart from one another up and down a series of deep ravines. The trail ran along the edge of a particularly deep one, providing breathtaking views of some of Indiana's finest scenery. Behind me, Hú Dié gave one of her banshee wails, and I knew she'd reached the first ravine. This section of the trail, called Pine Loop, had that effect on people.

I continued to hammer along the ravine's edge, pushing for every extra second I could get. I cruised through multiple switchbacks and over several small hills before I finally reached a steep, silty climb that I knew I would never be able to scale on a 'cross bike. This was where my cyclocross bike advantage ended, but I didn't care. It was the end of the road for me, anyway. I unclipped my feet and jumped off the bike, hauling it several yards off the trail into a stand of thick ferns and hiding it behind a log.

A moment later, I heard the hum of tires and the squeal of brakes as Hú Dié slowed to size up the silt-strewn hill.

"Pssst!" I said. "Hú Dié! Over here!"

She stopped for a second, removed her old hydration backpack, and tossed it to me as practiced. Then she grinned and turned her attention back to the hill. I expected her to shoulder her bike and run up the slope, but instead she switched to her granny gear and blasted forward, creeping up the hill as her rear tire sent a plume of chalky soil twenty yards behind her. It was slow going for her, but riding up the hill would ultimately be faster than running up it and taking the time to clip back into her pedals at the top. Also, whoever happened to be coming up behind her would have to wait until she crested the rise before attempting the climb themselves, unless they felt like being the recipient of a Category 5 dirt shower.

I heard the squeal of brakes again and figured it might be Jake coming up next, despite his poor starting position. I didn't stick around to find out, though. I had work to do.

I crouched low, keeping my head well below the tops of the ferns. I removed my own hydration backpack and carried it, along with Hú Dié's pack, into the forest.

I knew this area fairly well, having come here with Grandfather a couple of times to camp and hunt for morel mushrooms. Set into the hillside were numerous tiny caves, and I kept my eye out for one particular recess that was roughly the size of a bowling ball. It was above a bed of stinkhorn mushrooms, which smelled like ten-day-old garbage that had been rotting in the sun. I'd never seen a single animal track near that spot, and any hiker or mushroom hunter who happened past would also likely keep well away because of the putrid smell.

That was exactly what I was counting on.

I located the stinkhorn patch and, doing my best not to gag from the stench, opened both backpacks. From Hú Dié's pack, I withdrew a folding camp shovel. From mine, I removed a silk bag containing enough dragon bone to last Grandfather at least fifteen years.

I'd set aside ten years' worth at home, as Grandfather had instructed, and sent the rest off to PawPaw and Grandmaster Long. However, I couldn't keep myself from holding back an additional fifteen years' worth for Grandfather, in case he changed his mind. I was pretty sure PawPaw and Grandmaster Long wouldn't notice the difference, because I'd sent them each enough to last more than a hundred years. If Grandfather decided ten years from now that he wanted to stick around a little longer, he would be able to. If not, he could always send it to PawPaw or Grandmaster Long in the future.

I told no one my plan except Hú Dié. I couldn't pull this off alone. I figured if she was willing to take a bullet for me, my secret would be safe with her. We'd run through my plan twice when we rode here the other day with Ryan, who was none the wiser, and everything went smoothly then. I hoped it would go just as smoothly now.

I found the recess and shoved the dragon bone into it. I had done some research and learned that silk was resistant to mold and mildew, and most insects wouldn't eat it. The dragon bone would be secure inside the new bag I'd purchased. I had a feeling it would somehow suffocate over time or be ruined by condensation if I buried it in a sealed container.

I gathered up a few fist-sized rocks and plugged the recess opening; then I unfolded the shovel and sealed the gaps with soil I dug from beyond the stinkhorn bed. Finally, I kicked a layer of fallen leaves over the entire spot and stepped back to admire my work. No one would ever guess that the ground had been disturbed here, and once the leaves settled and the stinkhorns poked their nasty, slimy heads back into the air, people and animals alike would continue to steer clear. I scraped the dirt off the shovel and wiped it clean with leaves; then I folded it up, stuck it back in Hú Dié's pack, and headed for my bike. Someday I would have to return and mark the location with a GPS unit. If anything ever happened to those mushrooms, I might never find the dragon bone again.

I reached the bike a few minutes later and cautiously pushed it back to the trail. I didn't see any riders, and hadn't expected to. Even the slowest of the bunch would be well beyond this point by now. I slung my empty pack over one shoulder and Hú Dié's pack over the other, and then I picked up the bike and went cross-country on foot.

I hurried across the bike trail and headed down the side of the ravine. It was slick and slow going, and I fell more than once. I did my best not to travel down the hill in a straight line, to minimize the chance of anybody seeing any sort of trail I might be leaving behind. Fortunately, the forecast called for heavy rain that afternoon, and the sheets of water that typically flowed down these slopes would wash away even my deepest footprints and skid marks.

I reached the bottom and found the return leg of the mountain bike trail. Like most single-tracks, this trail was one long loop. Riders rode along the top of the ravine at the beginning, and they passed along here at the bottom of the ravine on their way back to the finish line in the parking lot, where the race began.

I rushed along the trail in the direction of the finish line until I came to a particularly tight bend that flowed around a gigantic boulder. I continued around the boulder, still carrying the bike, and rammed the front wheel into the huge rock with all my might. The front wheel didn't exactly taco, but it warped enough to make it unrideable. I felt bad about damaging Ryan's bike, but I needed an excuse for having stopped riding. I could have finished the race ahead of the others, of course, and no one would have known about my shortcut, but I was no cheat. I also had to give Hú Dié her pack back.

I heard the familiar hum of bike tires on the far side of the boulder and I shouted, "Rider down!"

Brakes squealed, and Hú Dié eased around the bend. She was covered in sweat and was panting like a tigress, but she was winning. I tossed her pack to her and she slipped it on; then she flashed a brilliant smile and blasted off like a rocket without saying a word. If her hand was bothering her, she didn't show it.

I grinned. The guys were going to be so angry when they got to the parking lot and found that they'd all been punked by a girl with a hole in her hand.

I heard another rider approaching, so I called out again, "Rider down!"

More brakes squealed, and Jake crept around the boulder.

"Phoenix?" he said. "What happened, bro? You okay?"

"I'm fine," I replied. "I couldn't make the stupid turn with this clunky 'cross bike and I crashed into the boulder. Looks like I'll be buying Ryan a new rim. You'd better keep moving, unless you want Iron Butterfly to embarrass you even more than she already has."

"Is that what *Hú Dié* means?" Jake asked. "Cool! Man, that girl can *ride*."

Tires hummed on the far side of the boulder, and I shouted once more, "Rider down!"

"Later days," Jake said, and he took off.

Ryan rounded the bend next. I was really impressed. His face was as red as a fire engine, and he was sweating so much that it looked as if a garden hose were connected to the underside of his helmet. I could detect a faint aroma of dragon bone coming from him, but it wasn't bad. Maybe he was finally on his way to severing the connection.

"You're doing great!" I said, encouraging him. "Keep it up!"

"I'll . . . try," Ryan huffed.

"Give it all you've got, my friend. I'm out of the race and Hú Dié is long gone, but Jake is only a few seconds ahead of you. Hunt him down and eat him for lunch!"

Ryan took a deep breath and gave one of his lion roars. He began to hammer. An instant later, he was gone.

The rest of the pack showed up, and I shouted my "rider down" warning several more times as the group came around the boulder, a few of the riders smirking when they saw my contorted front wheel. They passed, and I was about to begin walking toward the finish line when I heard another rider coming. I shouted my warning, and the little kid who'd been lined up next to Ryan at the beginning of the race teetered around the boulder.

"Don't stop pedaling!" I warned. "You'll fall over. Never stop moving forward."

The kid began to pedal harder. He picked up some speed and leveled out, regaining his balance. "Thanks," he huffed. "My parents . . . keep telling me . . . the same thing. Never stop . . . moving forward."

I smiled. "Anyone else behind you?"

"No . . . I'm last. I told my dad . . . I was too young to race against . . . you older guys."

"Sorry to disappoint you, but *I'll* be the one bringing up the rear in this race."

A huge grin stretched across his freckled cheeks, and he picked up even more speed. "Yes!" he shouted as he zipped past me. "Today is the day I beat *Phoenix*!"

I had to laugh. He was right. This would be the first time I'd ever crossed a finish line last, but I still couldn't help feeling like I'd won.

About the Author

Jeff Stone is the author of the hugely successful Five Ancestors books. When that series concluded, he wanted to write something different from another tale set in seventeenth-century China. However, he was reluctant to completely let go of kung fu or the characters he had grown to love, so he created an opportunity to update them to his own time. Jeff lives in Indiana with his wife and two children, and while he's active in several forms of bike racing, mountain biking is his favorite. Sadly, without dragon bone, he is aging at the standard rate.